STRAIGHT *from the* HEART

IRISH

Love Letters

Edited by Bridget Hourican

Gill & Macmillan

Gill & Macmillan
Hume Avenue, Park West, Dublin 12
with associated companies throughout the world
www.gillmacmillan.ie

Text copyright © 2011, Bridget Hourican
Design and format copyright © 2011, Teapot Press Ltd
ISBN 9780717150250

Produced by Teapot Press Ltd
Designed by: Tony Potter & Clare Barber
Edited by: Tara Gallagher & Catherine Gough
Picture research by: Ben Potter & Elizabeth Golding

Printed in the EU

This book is typeset in Optima and Perpetua

5 4 3 2 1

STRAIGHT
from the
HEART
IRISH
Love Letters

Contents

Introduction

The novelist J.G. Farrell, writing from London in 1973 to his girlfriend, Sarah Bond, in New York, ends his letter: 'I was in the public library the other day flicking through a dry and weighty volume of Victorian social history when I came on a love-letter addressed to 'Tony'. Naturally, I read it greedily. Actually, it was only half written … the unnamed girl was begging forgiveness for some unspecified unfaithfulness which had merely been "experimental" but that ever since "the first time on the camp bed" (!!!) she had really known that he was the only one. This is the only amusing thing that's happened to me.'

Farrell's find in the public library gives me the Russian doll effect: a love letter within a love letter within a book of love letters! And in his witty way Farrell nails the excitement of the find. Up from the dry and weighty past, pop these missives full of humour, affection, histrionics, and feeling, instantly familiar and accessible to the 21st century. "You do not know, you ugly thing, how much I love you" writes Wolfe Tone to his wife from France in 1797, showing himself the kind of affectionate, slagging Irishman that still exists today. Put it in textspeak - u dunno, u ugly thing, how much I luv u - and he could have sent it yesterday.

Katherine O'Shea

Or take Parnell's letter to Katherine O'Shea from Kilmainham Gaol in 1882: 'My own dearest Wifie … I am very comfortable here, and have a beautiful room facing the sun – the best in the prison … My only fear is about my darling Queenie … Your King.' Parnell in public life was commanding, austere, detached; one could imagine him writing very arrogant or very passionate love letters, but 'wifie' - 'Queenie'? It smacks of baby-talk. You couldn't make it up.

Literature is full of love letters, many funny and inspired. But only in real life would Michael Collins follow up a lovely lyrical passage to Kitty Kiernan, assuring her that she is 'not forgotten', with a testy aside to stop nagging him: 'I have

Michael Collins

many obligations, and don't forget that, even in the midst of them, I didn't let two days pass without writing. But I musn't mind, must I? However, perhaps I do mind.'

Nabokov put it best: 'Happy is the novelist who manages to preserve an actual love letter that he received when he was young within a work of fiction, embedded in it like a clean bullet in flabby flesh.' Note the pun on 'bullet': love letters are bulletins from the heart and the hand on the trigger should be shaking; the novelist's practised aim is too steady.

When I started compiling these love letters I expected a few things: I thought there would, inevitably, be generalised emotion - life imitating art. While the professional writers might avoid stock images of love, I expected the politicians, scientists, soldiers, and farmers to fall prey to the moon, stars, roses and other ritual metaphors. I imagined deep but inarticulate passion struggling through awkward phrases, and on the other end of the scale, rhetoric and pomposity as risible as Mr Collins' proposal in Pride and Prejudice. I expected that some of the women from the last few centuries, lacking the discipline of education and careers, might, like Emma Bovary, be in thrall to romantic novels, and liable to work themselves up to passionate frenzies, couched in overwrought, derivate language.

Well, I was confounded. There is very little generalised emotion in these letters – I thought I detected a hint in Oscar Wilde to his newly-wed wife: 'The air is full of the music of your voice, my soul and body no longer mine, but mingled in some exquisite ecstasy with yours'. This, to my ears, is a bit heavy on the aesthetics and lacks the fervent passion of his letters to Lord Alfred Douglas, but Wilde's grandson Merlin Holland writes that 'no one but a cynic could read the sole surviving letter that [Oscar] wrote to [Constance] and still maintain the marriage was a sham' so it may be that, unfortunately, I'm a cynic. The interpretation of love letters is after all subjective. Bernard Shaw's letter to the actress, Mrs Patrick Campbell, is showy rather than heartfelt, but it's too stylish and witty to be generalised. And Wilde and Shaw are great writers - the politicians, scientists, and unknowns don't even hint at generalised emotion; they are sincere, idiosyncratic, and articulate. Check out the masterly and humorous use of repetition in sheep-farmer Alexander Crawford's letter from the Australian outback: 'Do tell me more about yourself in your letters, fill them up with Lillie, commence with Lillie, end with Lillie, and fill the space between with the same subject, and you may add a postscript about her too, it will not be too much.'

The girlfriends and fiancées are nothing like Madame Bovary. Admittedly Annie Hutton does sound a little star-struck and novelettish at the start of her letter to her fiancé, the very famous and handsome balladeer Thomas Davis: 'I have perfect confidence in you, you are everything that is noble and good' – but by the end of the

Oscar Wilde

*Lord Alfred Bruce Douglas
by George Charles Beresford,
National Portrait Gallery.*

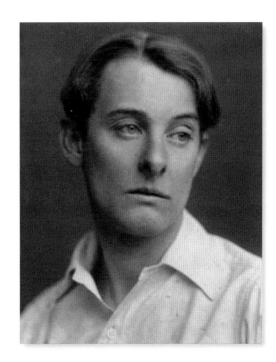

letter she is turning all her biting acuity on his elitist airs: 'I haven't quite forgiven yet your impertinent note, about being obliged to write gibberish, gibberish forsooth & pretty looking stuff, to enable your common readers I suppose to understand you.'

This note of humorous admonishment is characteristic of the female correspondents. These women, engaged or carrying on with great men, are as sharp-eyed as novelists, as psychologically acute as therapists. Mrs Patrick Campbell tells Shaw: 'I adore and at the same time detest your fears and tremblings and bewitching timidities'. Esther Vanhomrigh ('Vanessa') warns Swift (in her erratic spelling) that his policy of ignoring her isn't working: 'Once more I advise you if you have any regard for your quiete to allter your behaviour quickly for I do assure you I have too much spirrite to sitt down contented with this treatment.' Nora Barnacle replies to a hysterical letter from Joyce accusing her of cheating on him, with a scornful letter telling him to 'forget the ignorant Galway girl that came across [your] life'.

In the art of letter-writing, these women are the equals of these famous men, a fact which the men mostly recognised. Swift replied to 'Vanessa': 'If you write as you do, I shall come the seldomer on purpose to be pleased with your Letters, which I never look into without wondering how a Brat who cannot read, can possibly write so well' and Joyce to Nora: 'As long as I live I shall always remember the quiet dignity of that letter, its sadness and scorn, and the utter humiliation it caused me.'

A love-letter is seldom simply a missive saying 'I love you' (that's a Valentine's card) – the author generally has an agenda; he or she wants something from the recipient, whether it's marriage, attention, a change in behaviour, or sex. A few of the letters in this book were outstandingly successful in achieving their authors' aims: Violet Martin uses mockery, gossip and solicitude to get Edith Somerville's attention; Annie O'Donnell, nursery maid and Galway emigrant in Pittsburgh, isn't trying to seduce as a lover but to get across her wifely virtues of loyalty, reserve and steadfastness. Those two political activists, Hanna Sheehy and Frank Skeffington, dispatch at least as much recrimination and reproach as love, but then they aren't seeking to idealise but to lay the foundations for a fully equal, non-patriarchal

Esther Vanhomrigh, painting by Sir John Everett Millais,
Courtesy of National Museums, Liverpool.

partnership. Lillie Mathews wants to remind her sheep-farmer, Alexander Crawford, of his religious duties, and so to sweeten her lecture, she gets slyly up close: 'First try and think your little wife is on your knee with her arms round your neck and my head on your shoulder.'

Not everybody is so good at getting what they want. Mary Ann McCracken's letter to the United Irishman, Thomas Russell, is heart-rending: he's about to be executed, but she still can't break through and declare her love. Kitty Kiernan writing to Michael Collins is also painful to read – she is pulling out all the stops to get him to name the day, but he remains evasive. The young Iris Murdoch and Frank Thompson give the impression of playing poker, neither declaring their hand and waiting to see who blinks first, until it's too late. And the professional writers seem least successful at getting what (or who) they want - Swift, Sterne, Shaw, Yeats, Kavanagh and John Ford all fail in their aims to seduce the woman through prose.

It seems like a mass writers' failure, but you have to ask: is their objective really to get the girl? Or are they after the experience of rejection – seeking the uninterested muse as grist to the artists' mill? Haven't they unconsciously chosen just the women who will reject them? Kavanagh comes close to suggesting this, saying to Hilda Moriarty, who inspired 'Raglan Road': 'I like you because of your enchanting selfishness'. But the novelist George Moore is the only one to come right out and admit to Lady Cunard: 'You are a hard woman in many ways, but if you were less hard I don't think you would have held me captive such a long time.'

Writers exploit their lovers for art; this is what separates their letters from non-writers. Writers don't write 'better' letters – perhaps surprisingly, they have little advantage when it comes to conveying their feelings. The difference is that their letters are work-in-progress, extensions of their professional scripts. They try out scenarios and emotions which will turn up later in poems, plays, novels, and films.

This gives the letters of artists an extra layer. It's fascinating to read Yeats' letter to Maud Gonne in conjunction with 'The Circus Animals' Desertion', or Kavanagh to Hilda Moriarty with 'Raglan Road' in mind, or Sterne to Eliza Draper, thinking of *A Sentimental Journey*, or Ford to Maureen O'Hara after watching *The Quiet Man*.

Manet, Edouard (1832-1883): George Moore (1852-1933), 1873-79, Metropolitan Museum of Art, Pastel on canvas, 1929. Photograph by Malcolm Varon © 2011. Image copyright ©The Metropolitan Museum of Art / Art Resource / Scala, Florence.

There's that inter-textual dimension, so beloved of critics. But taken as discrete texts on their own evaluation, all these letters are fascinating. Each is unique and wonderful, each imperfect. Joyce has the sexual candour missing in the others - but is shot through with intensity and neediness. Parnell is probably writing the truth when he says he'd have remained childless without Katherine - but baby-talk? J.G. Farrell is very funny, but clearly a commitment-phobe; Kitty Kiernan is devoted but shouldn't she lighten up a bit and maybe read the papers? Is the brink of treaty negotiation really the time to be sending Collins page upon histrionic page?

Critics and psychologists like to depict love as a cultural construct, invented by courtly poets in the Middle Ages, and hyped in the 20th century to sell cards, movies, and products - 'What you call love was invented by guys like me to sell nylons' claims Don Draper in Mad Men. Obviously there's some truth to this – no way does everyone who writes 'I love you' on a Valentine's card actually mean it – but working on these letters has confirmed for me that in the ouroboros of art-imitating-life-imitating-art-imitating-life, then love has its origin in the real world before it's spun by artists and ad men.

Maud Gonne

The sixty people whose letters I reproduce here don't sound like characters in novels, plays, or films. When they do recall literary works, they actually pre-date them – for instance Sheridan's letter is reminiscent of Matthew Arnold's poem 'Dover Beach', but he wrote it half a century earlier.

If anything, love is an atavistic emotion that cuts through the cant of more acquired emotions like religious faith and patriotism. Take the 1916 signatory, Eamonn Ceannt, writing to his wife from Kilmainham Gaol the night before his execution: when he's on about Catholicism and nationalism he can sound rhetorical and pompous, but when he recalls their time together, he becomes direct, concrete, and

William Butler Yeats by George Charles Beresford
sepia-toned platinotype, 15 July 1911
© *National Portrait Gallery, London*

Éamonn Ceannt

poignant: 'My dearest "silly little Fanny"… my sweetheart of the hawthorn hedges and Summer's eves.' God and Country call forth rhetoric; love is personal.

Ceannt's letter, with its faith, nationalism, hawthorns and valedictory lines in Gaelic could only be Irish, but most of the letters are less instantly placeable. Is there a characteristically Irish love letter? There are characteristic Irish phrases; certainly Wolfe Tone's, already cited, seems quintessential. Swift writes to 'Stella' in the stream-of-consciousness of Finnegans Wake: 'Turn over [the page]. I had not room on t'other side to say that, so I did it on this: I fancy that's a good Irish blunder. Ah, why do not you go down to Clogher, nautinautinautideargirls; I dare not say nauti without dear; O, faith, you govern me.' And Michael Collins' use of the lyrical refrain 'you were not forgotten' recalls Gaelic poetry. However most of these letters – perhaps because written by the educated middle classes – don't use particularly Irish phrases or idioms. Daniel O'Connell's first language was Irish but there is nothing to distinguish his touching letter from an Englishman's of his age.

The evocation of place-names is more telling. In Irish literature, place-names are used hauntingly, almost as talismans. This is true of both languages, from early Gaelic poetry up to Paul Durcan, and has to do with the Gaelic tradition of fealty to local chieftains and terrains; with the traumatic transition from Gaelic to English and the attendant difficulty of rendering place-names (as dramatized by Brian Friel in Translations); and with a culture of emigration and homesickness. The evocation of place-names finds its way into some of these letters, most notably Joyce to Nora: 'I leave for Cork tomorrow morning but I would prefer to be going westward, towards those strange places whose names thrill me on your lips, Oughterard, Clare-Galway, Coleraine, Oranmore, towards those wild fields of Connacht in which God made to grow "my beautiful wild flower of the hedges, my dark-blue rain-drenched flower"'. This is very beautiful, and very conscious of the power being evoked. The emigrant Annie O'Donnell, writing at the same period, is plainer-spoken and less self-conscious, but what dignity and longing in her brief phrase, 'I was born in a little place called Spiddal about twenty miles from Galway City' - especially when we suspect she will never see Spiddal again. And Elizabeth Bowen, writing in 1957, beset with financial troubles, aware that her days in her ancestral home, Bowen's Court in Cork, are numbered, dwells on driving 'the last part of the road coming into Mallow from the Killarney side, being sucked – as it almost felt like – on and on under that long tunnel of trees in the darkening

twilight.' Three years later she had to sell Bowen's Court, saw it demolished, and lived the rest of her life in England.

These letters are written from beds and boudoirs, from lonely beaches and remote farms, from the trenches and the Blitz, from planes and hotels. One setting seems particularly Irish: prison. The man (or woman) facing execution and writing from the cell in anguish or exalted resignation to the loved one is a trope of love letters, but in few countries is it so standardized as in Ireland. I include here prison letters to and from Thomas Russell and Robert Emmet in 1803, Parnell in 1881, Ceannt and Plunkett in 1916, and Peadar Kearney in the War of Independence. Others of my correspondents, including Daniel O'Connell, Thomas MacDonagh, and Hanna Sheehy, were imprisoned but I haven't selected their gaol letters, and there are numerous other prisoners whose letters I haven't room for. It would not be hard to fill a book solely dedicated to Irish prison love letters.

With the changed political circumstances on both sides of the border, the political flavour has gone out of Irish love letters. And in a globalised world, Irish place-names may have lost some of their summoning power. What else has gone or changed? What kind of love letters are being written today? There are of course less and less being posted – anyone who now hand-writes and posts a love letter is either gifted graphically or deeply nostalgic. But as many love messages as ever fly out through texts and emails. Is this comparable? Of course there's no substitute for hand-writing on a page - an email floating in cyberspace, hosted on a server anywhere in the world, cannot be as personal or precious as a single hardcopy in the loved one's script. And a letter is a point of physical contact between lovers - the pages are touched (and kissed) by both, as the remarkable medieval Irish poem/letter, 'Aoibhinn, a leabhráin, do thriall', dramatizes. There's also a difference between the sanitised screen where corrections never show, and pen on paper where deletions and amendments reveal the tumult in the mind. (Check out Yeats' letter to Maud Gonne; an email would be much blander).

But the way we write is always changing and in each adjustment (the end of Latin as a lingua franca, the inventions of the printing press and the type-writer) something

Maud Gonne

is lost and something gained. I would guess that, simply because of ease of delivery, more written love messages are being sent today than at any time since the early 20th century. The postal service at the turn of the 20th century was so good that Joyce could send a letter to Nora in the morning to arrange to meet her that evening, and Frank Skeffington could rush one letter to Hanna Sheehy to catch the 4.30pm post, and immediately start another to catch the later post. Then came the widespread use of the telephone, and the downgrading of letters as vital means of communication. It's significant that in the later letters in this book, the correspondents are oceans apart; if they were in the same country, they'd pick up the phone. But for the past decade now it's been as easy, and cheaper, to text or email as phone. Perhaps many of these screen messages are bland, rushed and overly reliant on emoticons, but, equally, people are rising to the demands and limitations of the new forms: text messages require succinctness; emails give both sides of the correspondence, allowing lovers to check back on what they wrote earlier, which can add an interesting layer of self-consciousness and cross-referencing to their words.

The problem for future editors anthologizing a book of love-emails will be an embarrassment of riches - all those millions of messages preserved for perpetuity in cyberspace! With letters the terrain is beautifully uncluttered; fewer were written, many more got lost. The preservation of some of these letters, through prison and war and exile and revolution and scandal seems almost miraculous. How did the anonymous medieval poem survive turbulent centuries of war? All of Oscar Wilde's letters to his wife were destroyed by her family; how come one survived? How did Iris Murdoch's letters to Frank Thompson survive his sudden execution in Bulgaria? There is a mystery to the stubborn preservation of these single precious hardcopies. Mostly, of course, the recipient preserved the letter through love, and their descendants in their turn preserved it through love and fidelity. It is this loving act of preservation, as much as the immediacy of the emotions expressed, that gives these letters their arresting poignancy.

Maud Gonne and W. B. Yeats by John Nolan

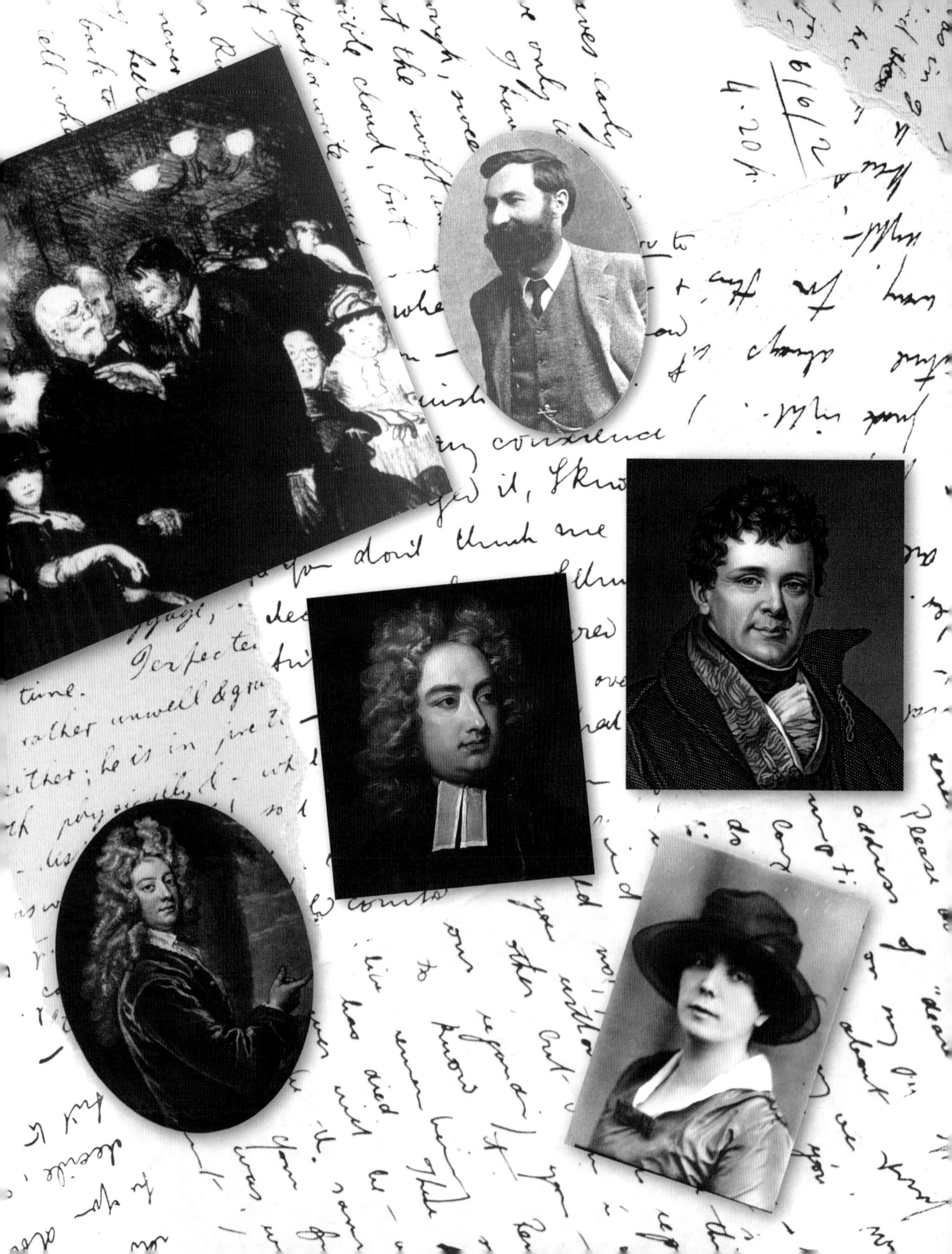

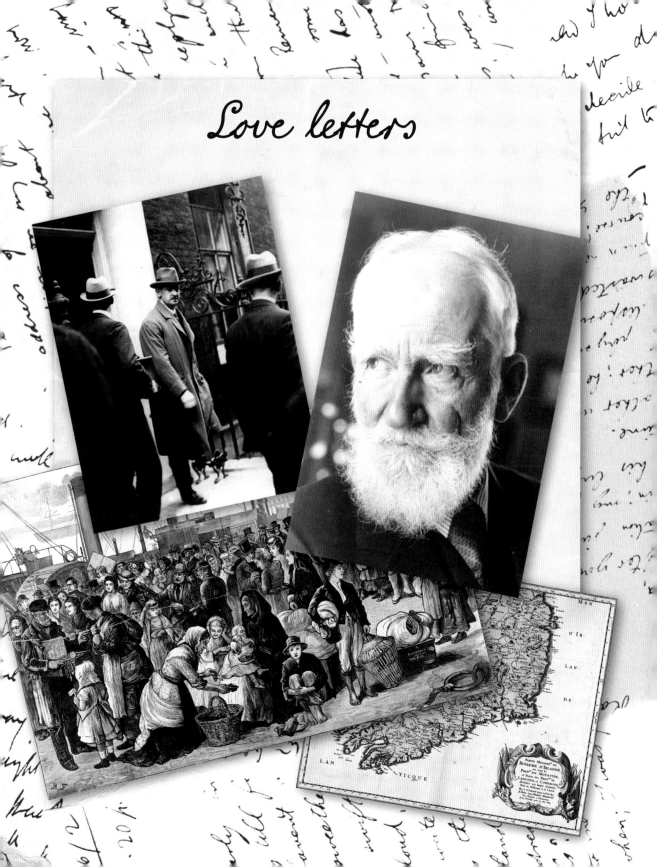

Love letters

Editor's note

Wherever possible I include both sides of the correspondence – if the correspondence is one-sided, it's because the other half is lost or unavailable. I have tried to be representative across period, gender and profession, but was unable to avoid a preponderance of letters from the busy period 1880–1921. This selection represents my personal choice from what is available.

I prefer to reprint the letters in full but since some of the letters are very long I have edited down in places. Ellipses between square brackets […] represent my cuts. Ellipses without brackets are as they appear in the original letter. Letters appear in their original spelling, grammar and syntax; my clarifications of archaic words or unusual spellings are in square brackets, as are translations from other languages.

I would have welcomed more letters in Irish but numerous inquiries seemed to confirm that there are few available. The consensus among those I consulted was that lovers in the Irish language tended to address each other in poetry, not prose. Since there are already many excellent anthologies of Irish poetry published and since I had ruled out including love poems in English, I was reluctant to include Irish love poems. However, I am grateful to Máirín Ní Dhonnchadha of NUI Galway for her insight into the link between courtly medieval 'dánta grádha' and amatory letters, and for her suggestion that I include the poem 'Aoibhinn, a leabhráin', as well as the letter from the Book of Leinster.

My great thanks to Pauraic Dempsey in the Royal Irish Academy for alerting me to the letters of scientists, composers, unknown soldiers and emigrants, and to Felix Larkin for putting me on the trail of George Moore, Iris Murdoch and the Sheehy-Skeffingtons. Patrick Geoghegan read and smartened the introduction and steered me tactfully away from my first choices of title. John Stephenson read the manuscript through, proofed excellently, and added wonderfully to the biographical information on the correspondents. Thanks to Catherine Gough and Tara Gallagher for their judicious edit. Finally, my great thanks to James McGuire and James Quinn, editors of the *Dictionary of Irish Biography* – I do not think these love letters would have been possible without the *Dictionary*.

Finn, Bishop of Kilare, to Áed mac Crimthainn, c.1160

The earliest known letter in Irish, written on the margin of the 12th-century *Book of Leinster*, is in the language of love, but is not apparently a love letter. It's a short note from Finn Úa Gormáin, Bishop of Kildare, to Áed mac Crimthainn, historian and scribe of the *Book of Leinster*. It starts off mildly mocking, with Finn extravagantly crediting five kinds of wisdom to Áed, and then segues into an ostensible love poem, praising Áed's beauty and longing for his presence. To us, it seems extraordinary language from a bishop, but in the Gaelic world men had less inhibitions about praising male beauty and making emotional addresses. Bards frequently fetishized the beauty of the king or lord, and Finn's is apparently routine language of friendship for the 12th-century. Is it worth quoting in a book of love letters? Yes, because few letters from the Gaelic world have survived, and it's striking that this, the earliest extant letter, employs what we would call the language of sensual love. And in Gaelic literature, friendship and love are not sharply differentiated – the story of Cúchulainn and Ferdia is at least as emotional as that of Diarmuid and Gráinne.

An early map of Leinster, Munster and Connaught.

Betha 7 sláinte o Fhind epscop (.i. Cilli Dara) do Aed mac Crimthainn do ḟir leigind ardrig Leithi Moga (.i. Nuadat) 7 do chomarbu Choluim meic Crimthaind 7 do phrimsenchaid Laigen ar gaes 7 eolas 7 trebaire lebur 7 fessa 7 foglomma 7 scribthar dam deired in sceoil bicse

cu cinte duit a Aed amnais
a fir cosinn aeb ollmais
cian gar dom beith it hingnais
mían dam do bith im comgnais.

Tucthar dam duanaire Meic Lonain co faiccmis a cialla na nduan filet ann.
et Uale in Christo.

[Life and health from Bishop Finn [of Kildare] to Áed mac Crimthainn,
lector of the great king of Leth Moga (Nuadat) and coarb [successor] of Colum mac
Crimthainn, and chief historian of Leinster for wisdom and knowledge and book
lore and science and learning. And let the end of this little tale written for me.

O keen Áed, know for sure,
Man of great beauty,
However long I am without you
My wish is to have you with me.

Let the poem-book of mac Lonáin be given to me that we may see the meanings of
the poems that are in it. And go in Christ.]

[Letter written on the lower margin of folio 206 of the 12th-century codex known as the Book of Leinster *and as*
The Book of Nuachonbgáil. *Translation: Máirín Ní Dhonnchadha.]*

Anonymous to 'the Lady with a Book', c.1350–1750

Lovers in the Gaelic world did not address each other in prose – or at least no one has been able to source me any prose love letters. It's significant that in the preceding letter Bishop Finn began in prose but turned to verse to write of love/friendship. In Volume 4 of the *Field Day Anthology*, Máirín Ní Dhonnchadha has pointed out a possible, intriguing link between the medieval *dánta grádha* (courtly love poems) and amatory letters. Nowhere does this link seem more explicit than in the following poem, which presumably accompanied the gift of a book. The anonymous writer is sending his lover, or muse, a book and is envying his gift its proximity to the lady. She is described in terms too good to be true; with her youth, red lips, grey eyes, pale skin and long legs she seems as unreal as a Hollywood pin-up. But the play on the book/poem's physicality is marvellous – the lovers can't meet, but this object, touched by both their hands, connects them. The writer's envy of the book, which he anthropomorphises, is comical and touching. This poem reminds us that lovers used to seal letters with a kiss – in the 20th century signing off with the acronym S.W.A.L.K – and the recipient would then kiss the page on delivery. No other letter in this book invests so much in the page's physicality, but then this was written in the Middle Ages, when poor transport made separation between lovers more final and the letter's 'journey' more vivid, and when paper was rarer, bulkier and more physically present.

Sir Frederic William Burton (1816–1900) Hellelil and Hildebrand, the Meeting on the Turret Stairs, *1864. Collection National Gallery of Ireland Photo © National Gallery of Ireland*

Aoibhinn, a leabhráin, do thriall
i gceann ainnre na gciabh gcam;
truagh gan tusa im riocht i bpéin
is mise féin ag dul ann.

A leabráin bhig, aoibhinn duit
ag triall mar a bhfuil mo ghrádh;
an béal loinneardha mar chrú
do-chífe tú, 's an déad bán

Do-chífe tusa an rosg glas,
do-chífir fós an bhas tláith;
biadh tú, 's ni bhiadh-sa, far-raor!
taobh ar thaobh 's an choimhgheal bhláith

Do-chífe tú an mhala chaol
's an bhráighe shaor sholas shéimh,
's an ghruaidh dhrithleannach mar ghrís
do chonnarc i bhfís a-réir.

An com sneachtaidhe seang slán
dá dtug mise grádh gan chéill,
's an troigh mhéirgheal fhadúr bhán
do-chífe tú lán do sgréimh.

An glór taidhiúir síthe séimh
do chuir mise I bpéin gach laoi
Cluinfir, is ba haoibhinn duid;
uch gan mo chuid bheith mar taoi!

Pleasant journey, little book
To that gay gold foolish head!
Though I wish that you remained
And I travelled in your stead.

Gentle book, 'tis well for you,
Hastening where my darling rests:
You will see the crimson lips,
You will touch the throbbing breasts.

You will see the dear grey eye.
On you will that hand alight —
Ah, my grief 'tis you not I
Will rest beside her warm at night.

You will see the slender brows
And the white nape's candle-gleam,
And the fond flickering cheeks of youth
That I saw last night in dream.

And the waist my arms would clasp
And the long legs and stately feet
That pace between my sleep and me
With their magic you will meet.

And the soft pensive sleepy voice
Whose echoes murmur in my brain
Will bring you rest — 'tis well for you!
When shall I hear that voice again?

[Translation: Frank O'Connor, Kings, Lords and Commons (New York: Knopf, 1959).]

William Congreve and Arabella Hunt

William Congreve, engraving after Sir Godfrey Kneller.

24-year-old William Congreve, who has just scored a triumph on the London stage with his first play, is writing to his mistress, the singer Mrs Arabella Hunt. She has demanded his presence in Epsom but he is ill in Windsor and, in a witty conceit comparing his nurse to an ass, explains that he can only 'journey towards health on that animal' and that because of the 'slowness of that beast' (i.e. the poor quality of the nursing), his advance is slow. He hopes instead that Arabella will come to him, but his rueful last line – surely an ironic comment on the efficacy of prayer – suggests he knows that she won't.

Smith, I; After Kneller, G, Sir: 'Mrs Arabella Hunt (1662–1705)'
© The Hunterian, University of Glasgow

WINDSOR, JULY 26, 1694

Angel,

There can be no stronger Motive to bring me to Epsom, or to the North of Scotland, or to Paradise, than your being in any of those Places; for you make every Place alike Heavenly where-ever you are. And I believe if any thing could cure me of a natural Infirmity, seeing and hearing you would be the surest Remedy; at least, I should forget that I had any thing to complain of while I had so much more Reason to rejoice. I should certainly (had I been at my own Disposal) have immediately taken Post for Epsom, upon Receipt of your Letter: but I have a Nurse here, who has Dominion over me; a most unmerciful She-Ass. Balaam was allow'd an Angel to his Ass; I'll pray, if that will do any good, for the same Grace. I would have set out upon my Ass to have waited upon you, but I was afraid I should have been a tedious while in coming, having great Experience of the Slowness of that Beast: For you must know, I am making my Journey towards Health upon that Animal, and I find I make such slow Advances, that I despair of arriving at you, or any great Blessing, till I am

capable of using some more expeditious means.
I could tell you of a great Inducement to bring
you to this Place, but I am sworn to Secrecy;
however, if you were here, I would contrive to
make you of the Party. I'll expect you, as a good
Christian may every thing that he devoutly prays
for. I am

Your everlasting Adorer
W. Congreve

Anne Bracegirdle

This is the only surviving love letter from Congreve, who never married, but had three great loves in his life: Arabella Hunt, the actress Anne Bricegirdle and Lady Henrietta Godolphin, daughter of the Duke of Marlborough. He caused scandal when he bequeathed all his property to Henrietta and named her husband as executor, but it was probably a discreet means of endowing the daughter she bore him. His epitaph in Westminster Abbey, composed by Henrietta, can be considered a kind of love letter. The last line commends his writings to the future, but only his comic masterpiece, *The Way of the World*, is still much read and performed, though it flopped on its first performance on the 12th of March 1700.

Mr. William Congreve

Dyed jan the 19th 1728 Aged 56. And was buried near this place, To whose most Valueable Memory this Monument is Sett up by HENRIETTA, Duchess of MARLBOROUGH as a mark how dearly, SHE remember the happiness and Honour She enjoyed in the Sincere Friendshipp of so worthy and Honest a Man, Whose Virtue Candour and Witt gained him the love and Esteem of the present Age and whose Writings will be the Admiration of the Future.

[William Congreve, Letters & Documents, collected and edited by John C. Hodges, Harcourt, Brace and World, 1964.]

Jonathan Swift and Jane Waring ('Varina')

Jonathan Swift is supposed to be persuading his 'Varina' to marry him but he can't lay off berating her. Just ordained, but festering in an obscure Antrim parish and, at 29, still unpublished and three decades away from the great fame of *Gulliver's Travels*, Swift has his heart but no fortune to offer Jane Waring ('Varina'), daughter of the Archdeacon of Dromore. She is having reservations – her health, his finances – and he can't forgive her vacillation. This letter has stately passages about the nature of love and the superiority of instinct over society's 'empty forms', but his innate irascibility keeps breaking through. He calls her affected and cold, a hardened flirt who enjoys intrigue, and he allows his hurt to tip into misogyny towards 'those who have been these 5000 years using us ill'. He doesn't praise her – except for the 'pity' which first drew him, but which, he now insinuates, was false. Is this his idea of a seduction letter? Is he – in an early example of reverse-psychology pick-up techniques – trying to 'diss' or 'neg' her so that she doubts herself and becomes dependent on him? Does he expect this to work? Does he want it to work? Or is he unconsciously sabotaging his own suit because of an aversion to marriage?

[CARRICKFERGUS] APRIL 29, 1696

Madam,

Impatience is the most inseparable quality of a lover, and indeed of every person who is in pursuit of a design wheron he conceives his greatest happiness or misery to depend. It is the same thing in war, in courts, and in common business. Every one who hunts after pleasure, or fame, or fortune, is still restless and uneasy till he has hunted down his game: and all this is not only very natural, but something reasonable too; not to blame in looking after a cure. I find myself infected with this malady, and am easily vain enough to believe it has some very good reasons to excuse it. For indeed, in my case, there are some circumstances which will admit pardon for more ordinary disquiets. That dearest object upon which all my prospects of happiness entirely depend, is in perpetual danger to be removed for ever from my sight. Varina's life is daily wasting; and though one just and honourable action would furnish health to her, and unspeakable happiness to us both, yet some power that repines at human felicity has that influence to hold her continually doating on her cruelty, and me upon the cause of it. This fully convinces me of what we are told, that the miseries of life are all beaten out in his own anvil. Why was I so foolish to put my hopes and fears into the power or management of another? Liberty is doubtless the most valuable blessing of life; yet we are fond to fling it away on those who have been these 5000 years using us ill. […]

I am a villain if I have not been po[u]ring this half hour over the paper merely for want of something to say to you: – or is it rather that I have so much to say to you, that I know not where to begin, though at last 'tis all very likely to be arrant repetition?

[…]You have now had time to consider my last letter, and to form your own resolutions upon it. I wait your answer with a world of impatience; and if you think fit I should attend you before my journey, I am ready to do it. […] how far you will stretch the point of your unreasonable scruples to keep me here, will depend upon the strength of the love you pretend for me.

[…] 'Tis true you have known sickness longer than you have me, and therefore perhaps you are more loath to part with it as an older acquaintance: But listen to what I here solemnly protest, by all that can be witness to an oath, that if I leave this kingdom before you are mine, I will endure the utmost indignities of fortune rather than ever return again, though the king would send me back his deputy. And if it must be so, preserve yourself, in God's name, for the next lover who has those qualities you love so much beyond any of mine, and who will highly admire you for those advantages which shall never share any esteem from me. Would to Heaven you were but a while sensible of the thoughts into which my present distractions plunge me: they hale [beat] me a thousand ways, and I am not able to bear them. 'Tis so, by Heaven: the love of Varina is of more tragical consequence than her cruelty. Would to God you had hated and scorned me from the beginning. It was your pity opened the first way to my misfortune; and now your love is finishing my ruin: and is it so then? In one fortnight I must take eternal farewel of Varina; and (I wonder) will she weep at parting, a little to justify her poor pretences of affection to me? And will my friends still continue reproaching me for the want of gallantry, and neglecting a close siege? How comes it that they all wish us married together [;] they know my circumstances and yours extremely well, and I am sure love you too much, if it be only for my sake, to wish you any thing that might cross your interests or your happiness?

Surely, Varina, you have but a very mean opinion of the joys that accompany a true, honourable, unlimited love; yet either nature and our ancestors have hugely deceived us, or else all other sublunary things are dross in comparison. Is it possible you can be yet insensible to the prospect of rapture and delight so innocent and so exalted? Trust me, Varina, Heaven has given us nothing else worth the loss of a thought. Ambition, high appearance, friends, and fortune, are all tasteless and insipid when they come in competition; yet millions of such glorious minutes are we perpetually losing, for ever losing, irrevocably losing, to gratify empty forms and wrong notions, and affected coldnesses and peevish humour. These are the unhappy incumbrances which we who are distinguished from the vulgar do fondly create to torment ourselves. […] By Heaven, Varina, you are more experienced, and have less virgin innocence than I. Would not your conduct make one think you were highly skilled in all the little politic methods of intrigue? Love, with the gall of too much discretion, is a thousand times worse than with none at all. […] To resist the violence of our inclinations in the beginning, is a strain of self-denial that may have some pretences to set up for a virtue: but when they are grounded at first upon reason, when they have taken firm root and are grown up to a height, 'tis folly – folly as well as injustice, to withstand their dictates; for this passion has a property particular to itself, to be most commendable in its extremes, and 'tis as possible to err in the excess of piety as of love.

These are the rules I have long followed with you, Varina; and had you pleased to imitate them, we should both have been infinitely happy. The little disguises, and affected contradictions of your sex, were all (to say the truth) infinitely beneath persons of your pride and mine; paltry maxims that they are,

Swift D.D.

calculated for the rabble of humanity. Oh Varina, how imagination leads me beyond myself and all my sorrows! 'Tis sunk and a thousand graves lie open! — No, Madam, I will give you no more of my unhappy temper, though I derive it all from you.

Farewell, Madam, and may love make you a while forget your temper to do me justice. Only remember that if you still refuse to be mine, you will quickly lose, for ever lose, him that is resolved to die as he has lived, all yours,

Jon. Swift

She didn't say yes, but she didn't say no either. Even after his return to London, the affair dragged on, for her at least, another four years. In a letter that has not survived she wrote asking why his behaviour towards her was changed. He replied, on the 4th of May 1700, with a savage letter, taunting her with her former reservations about his small fortune and her poor health, and evoking an unpleasant picture of their married life: she would live parsimoniously, suffering his didacticism and 'rugged humour'.

Gulliver runs afoul of the Lilliputians.

Jonathan Swift and Esther Johnson ('Stella')

Stella, Sir John Everett Millais / Manchester Art Gallery, The Bridgeman Art Library.

There were to be no more marriage proposals from Swift, not even to Esther Johnson ('Stella'), though he told one of her suitors: 'If my fortunes and humour served me to think of that state [marriage], I should certainly, among all the persons of the earth, make your choice; because I never saw that person whose conversation I entirely valued but hers.' It was not surprising he valued her conversation since he had formed it. They met in Surrey when 'Stella' was a child and he in his twenties; she became Galatea to his Pygmalion. In 1700 he invited her to Dublin to live near him and she never married. People began gossiping about their relationship during his lifetime and haven't stopped since. Was he actually her cousin, or her uncle? Was there a secret marriage? Were they ever even alone in a room together?

We don't know. All we have are 65 of his letters, written between 1710 and 1713, when she was turning thirty and he was in his forties and delighted to be living in London as chief Tory propagandist. These letters minutely record his daily activities and read like diary entries (they were eventually published as *A Journal to Stella*). Are they love letters? Not conventionally – they aren't even addressed exclusively to Stella but also to her companion Mrs Dingley (the acronym 'MD' stands for 'my dears', while he calls himself 'Presto'). Presto's attitude towards his 'MD' is often ribald – he looks forward to whipping them and 'banging [their] bones' and he's always writing to his 'saucy sluts' from bed – but mostly he's avuncular. Stella was the only person to whom he was invariably affectionate; her adulation relaxed his mind. In this extract from a much longer letter, he's so relaxed he slips into stream-of-consciousness; the erratic flitting from subject to subject and the nonsense compound words look forward to Joyce. *A Journal to Stella* is Swift communing with himself. She was more amanuensis than muse.

LONDON, Dec. 9, 1710
[Letter 11]

So, young women, I have just sent my tenth [letter] to the post-office, and, as I told you, have received your seventh (faith, I am afraid I mistook, and said your sixth, and then we shall be all in confusion this month.) Well, I told you I dined with Lord Abercorn to-day; and that is enough till by and bye; for I must go write idle things, and twittle twattle. What's here to do with your little MD's? and so I put this by for a while. 'Tis now late, and I can only say MD is a dear, saucy rogue, and what then? Presto loves them the better.
[…]
13th [Dec] […] Well, these saucy jades take up so much of my time with writing to them in a morning; but, faith, I am glad to see you whenever I can: a little snap and away; and so hold your tongue, for I must rise: not a word, for your life. How nowww? So, very well; stay till I come home, and then, perhaps, you may hear further from me. And where will you go to-day, for I can't be with you ladies? It is a rainy, ugly day. I'd have you send for Walls, and go to the Dean's; but don't play small games when you lose. You'll be ruined by Manilio, Basto, the queen, and two small trumps, in red. I confess 'tis a good hand against the player: but then there are Spadilio, Punto, the king, strong trumps, against you, which, with one trump more, are three tricks ten ace: for, suppose you play your Manilio--Oh, silly, how I prate, and can't get away from this MD in a morning! Go, get you gone, dear naughty girls, and let me rise.
[…]
14th [Dec]. Stay, I'll answer some of your letter this morning in bed: let me see; come and appear, little letter. Here I am, says he: and what say you to Mrs. MD this morning fresh and fasting? Who dares think MD negligent? I allow them a fortnight; and they give it me. I could fill a letter in a week; but it is longer every day; and so I keep it a

Jonathan Swift and Esther Johnson ('Stella')

Jonathan Swift

40

fortnight, and then 'tis cheaper by one half. I have never been giddy, dear Stella, since that morning: I have taken a whole box of pills, and kecked at [retched over] them every night, and drank a pint of brandy at mornings. Oh then, you kept Presto's little birthday: would to God I had been with you! I forgot it, as I told you before. REdiculous, madam? I suppose you mean rIdiculous: let me have no more of that; 'tis the author of the Atalantis's spelling. I have mended it in your letter. And can Stella read this writing without hurting her dear eyes? O, faith, I am afraid not. Have a care of

Swift's death mask

those eyes, pray, pray, pretty Stella. 'Tis well enough what you observe, that, if I writ better, perhaps you would not read so well, being used to this manner; 'tis an alphabet you are used to: you know such a pot-hook makes a letter; and you know what letter, and so and so. I'll swear he told me so, and that they were long letters too; but I told him it was a gasconnade [bravado] of yours, etc. I am talking of the Bishop of Clogher, how he forgot. Turn over [the page]. I had not room on t'other side to say that, so I did it on this: I fancy that's a good Irish blunder. Ah, why do not you go down to Clogher, nautinautinautideargirls; I dare not say nauti without dear: O, faith, you govern me. But, seriously, I'm sorry you don't go, as far as I can judge at this distance. No, we would get you another horse; I will make Parvisol [their servant?] get you one. I always doubted that horse of yours: prythee sell him, and let it be a present to me. My heart aches when I think you ride him. Order Parvisol to sell him, and that you are to return me the money: I shall never be easy until he is out of your hands. Faith, I have dreamt five or six times of horses stumbling since I had your letter. If he can't sell him, let him run this winter. Faith, if I was near you, I would whip your ---- to some tune, for your grave, saucy answer about the Dean and Johnsonibus; I would, young women. And did the Dean preach for me? Very well. Why, would they have me stand here and preach to them?

[...] But what now, you saucy sluts? all this written in a morning, and I must rise and go abroad. Pray stay till night: do not think I will squander mornings upon you, pray, good madam. Faith, if I go on longer in this trick of writing in the morning, I shall be afraid of leaving it off, and think you expect it, and be in awe. Good-morrow, sirrahs, I will rise [...] At night ... Hussy, Stella, you jest about poor Congreve's eyes; you do so, hussy; but I'll bang your bones, faith.

[...]

23rd [Dec.] [...] Good-night, little dears both, and be happy; and remember your poor Presto, that wants you sadly, as hope saved. Let me go study, naughty girls, and don't keep me at the bottom of the paper. O, faith, if you knew what lies on my hands constantly, you would wonder to see how I could write such long letters; but we'll talk of that some other time. Good-night again, and God bless dear MD with His best blessings, yes, yes, and Dingley and Stella and me too, etc.

Jonathan Swift and Esther Vanhomrigh ('Vanessa')

Swift writes to Stella of dining with Mrs Vanhomrigh, the widow of a Dublin merchant, but doesn't admit to taking coffee with her daughter 'in the sluttery' [his name for their parlour]. But then he has no idea this young woman will pursue him for the rest of her life. Esther Vanhomrigh's ('Vanessa') first extant letter to Swift, written in 1712 when she was 24, begins, 'Had I a Correspondant [sic] in China I might have had an answer by this time' and this complaint sets the tone for all her future letters. She constantly reproaches him for not writing, not thinking of her, not coming to see her. In 1714 Swift, now out of favour in party politics, returned to Ireland as Dean of St Patrick's, and 'Vanessa' followed him, setting up house in Celbridge, Kildare, and taking lodgings in Dublin. In this typically histrionic, erratically spelled letter, she sounds her usual refrains – 'reproving you when you behave yourself so wrong' and threatening to bring him to her 'by force' if 'you will not come of your self'. But if she nagged, she was also witty, lively and, as she writes here, full of 'spirrite' and 'frankness', and was too much in love to deliver on her threats; by the end of this tumultuous, badly spelled letter she is assuring him that whatever time he visits, he will be well-received.

Vanessa, by Millais,
Courtesy of National Museums Liverpool.

[To Dr Swift 1719–20?]

Is it possible that again, you will do, the very same thing I warned you of so lately. I
believe you thought I only rallyed when I told you the other night that I wou'd
pester you with letters. (did not I know you very well I should think you knew little
of the world, to imagine that a woman would not keep her word
when ever she promised any thing that was malicious. had not you better a

thousand times, throw away one hour, at some time or other of the day. then to be interrupted in your business at this rate for I know tis as impossible for you to burn my letters, without reading them. as tis for me to avoid reproving you when you behave yourself so wrong.) once more I advise you if you have any regard for your quiete to allter your behaviour quickly for I do assure you I have too much spirrite to sitt down contented with this treatment now because I love frankness extreamly I here tell you that I have determined to try all manner of humain artes to reclaim you and if all those fail I am resolved to have recourse to the black one which [it] is said never do[e]s now see what inconveainences you will bring both me and your self into. pray think more calmely of it is it not much better to come of your self than to be brought by force & that perhaps when you have the most agreaible ingagement [agreeable engagement] in the world for when I under take any thing I don't love to do it be halves (but there is one thing falls out very ruckiley [luckily] to you which is that of all the pasions revenge hurryes me least so that you have it yet in your power to turne all this furry [fury] in to good humer, and depend upon it and more I assure you come at what time you pleas you can never fail of being very well received).

Swift was strongly attracted but alarmed at the thought of public scandal and hurt to Stella, as he explains in the long poem, 'Cadenus and Vanessa'. In his letters to Vanessa, he was frequently circumspect and impatient – to an early reproach that he was ignoring her, he wrote coldly: 'I had your last spleenatick Letter: I told you when I left England, I would endeavour to forget every thing there, and would write as seldom as I could' and he tried to put her off following him to Ireland, warning that he would see her 'very seldom'. Except when writing in French – which language had an amorous effect on him – he did not praise her, but this reply to her above letter shows him in a softened, affectionate, even flirtatious mood. Everything about Swift's relations with women is mysterious – we don't know if he slept with Vanessa, but his tone is certainly more sexual than with Stella.

[1720?] To Miss Hessy Vanhom[r]i

If you write as you do, I shall come the seldomer on purpose to be pleased with your Letters, which I never look into without wondring how a Brat who cannot read, can possibly write so well. You are mistaken; send me a Letter without your Hand on the outside, and I hold you a Crown, I shall not read it. But raillery a Part, I think it inconvenient for a hundred Reasons that I should make your House a sort of constant dwelling place. I will certainly come as often as I conveniently can, but my Health and the perpetuall run of ill Weather hinders me from going out in the morning, and my afternoons are taken up I know not how, that I am in rebellion with a dozen People beside your self, for not seeing them. For the rest, you need make use of no other Black Art besides your Ink, 'tis a pity your Eyes are not black, or I would have said the same of them: but you are a white Witch, and can do no Mischief. If you have employed any of your Art on the Black Scarf, I defy it, for one reason; guess.

Adieu for Dr P— is come in to see me

He is surely leading her on here, and weakening his demand that she 'Settle [her] Affairs, and quit this scoundrel Island'. Vanessa continued to reproach that he made her 'live a life like a languishing Death' but she couldn't leave him. However, she got revenge by excluding him from her Will in favour of the other great 18th–century Irish man of letters, George Berkeley. She died in 1723, five years before Stella. Swift lived on until 1745 and had no more romantic friendships to tease biographers with.

George Berkeley

[The Correspondence of Jonathan Swift, edited by Harold Williams, Oxford University Press, 1963; Jonathan Swift, Journal to Stella *(1766–1768).]*

Laurence Sterne and Eliza Draper

Fifty-four-year-old Anglican clergyman and Europe's latest literary sensation, Laurence Sterne, is either infatuated beyond belief, indulging in high camp, or both, in this hilarious, histrionic letter to his young married muse, Eliza Draper (22). After a lifetime of obscurity, he is enjoying huge success as the author of *Tristram Shandy*. Eliza and he have just met and she is about to re-join her husband in India. The thought of the impending separation is too much – he offers to pay her to remain in England. He hardly knows her – why is he so obsessed? Because she was pretty, flirtatious and, most importantly, sickly. Sterne, himself tubercular, believed, as he writes here, that illness arises 'from the affliction of the mind' and is a sign of sensitivity, or (his favourite word) sentimentality. Health – his, Eliza's, his wife's, her husband's – is the main subject of this letter, which takes amazing liberties: in one breath he's offering his wife and daughter to 'carry you in pursuit of health to Montpelier'; the next he's happily killing off his wife, widowing Eliza and offering himself as her new husband in a marriage that won't, of course, last long (he doubles the already great disparity in their ages, making himself 'ninety-five in constitution'). The Victorians were appalled by Sterne's dealings with women – as he writes here, Eliza was 'not the first woman by many' – but whether he is predominantly joking or fantasizing in his amatory letters, he is surely not to be taken at his word.

[March 1767]

I Wish to God, Eliza, it was possible to postpone the voyage to India for another year, for I am firmly persuaded within my own breast, that thy husband could never limit thee with regard to time ---

[…] But, Eliza, if thou art so very ill, still put off all thoughts of returning to India this year --- write to your husband -- tell him the truth of your case --- if he is the generous humane man you describe him to be, he cannot but applaud your conduct --- I am credibly informed, that his repugnance to your living in England arises only from the dread which has enter'd his brain, that thou mayest run him in debt, beyond thy appointments, and that he must discharge them --- That such a creature should be sacrificed, for the paltry consideration a few hundreds, is too, too hard! Oh! my child, that I could with propriety indemnify him for every charge, even to the last mite, that thou hast been of to him! With joy would I give him my whole subsistence, nay, sequester my livings, and trust the treasures heaven has furnish'd my head with, for a future subsistence ---

You owe much, I allow, to your husband; you owe something to appearances, and the opinion of the world; but, trust me, my dear, you owe much likewise to yourself --- Return therefore from Deal if you continue ill: I will prescribe for you gratis. You are not the first woman by many, I have done so for with success --- I will send for my wife and daughter, and they shall carry you in pursuit of health to Montpelier, the wells of Bancer's, the Spaw, or whither thou wilt; thou shalt direct them, and make parties of pleasure in what corner of the world fancy points out to you. We shall fish upon the banks of Arno, and lose ourselves in the sweet labyrinths of its vallies, and then thou should'st warble to us, as I have once or twice heard thee 'I'm lost. I'm lost,' but we should find thee again, my Eliza ---

Of a similar nature to this, was your physician's prescription 'ease, gentle exercise, the pure southern air of France or milder Naples, with the society of friendly, gentle beings' --- Sensible man, he certainly enter'd into your feelings, he knew the fallacy of medicine to a creature, whose ILLNESS HAS ARISEN FROM THE AFFLICTION OF HER MIND--Time only, my dear, I fear you must trust to, and have your reliance on; may it give you the health so enthusiastic a votary to the charming goddess deserves ---

Talking of widows --- pray, Eliza, if ever you are such, do not think of giving yourself to some wealthy nabob, because I design to marry you myself --- My wife cannot live long-- she has sold all the provinces in France already, and I know not the woman I should like so well for her substitute, as yourself --- 'Tis true, I am ninety-five in constitution, and you but twenty-five; rather too great a disparity this! but what I want in youth, I will make up in wit and good humour --- Not Swift so lov'd his Stella, Scarron his Maintenon, or Waller his Sacharissa*, as I will love and sing thee, my wife elect --- all those names, eminent as they were, shall give place to thine, Eliza. Tell me in answer to this, that you approve and honour the proposal; and that you would (like the Spectator's mistress) have more joy in putting on an old man's slipper, than associating with the gay, the voluptuous, and the young --- Adieu, my Simplicia ---

Yours
TRISTRAM

[From his most famous novel; Sterne usually signed himself 'Brahmin' or 'Yorick' to Eliza.]

Eliza didn't take him seriously, but sailed for India on the 3rd of April 1767. By then he didn't require her presence but could feed his infatuation through extravagant journal entries; on the 19th of April he records that he is unable to talk of Eliza 'without bursting into tears a dozen different times' (how can one burst into tears 'differently'?). Eliza was now so much a figment of imagination that when reality – her own words – intruded he withdrew: in July her letters from India reached him; a few days later he abandoned the journal. Many of the feelings she called forth went into his final masterpiece, *A Sentimental Journey*, published early the next year, in February 1768.

He wasn't exaggerating his poor health, or Eliza's. He died three weeks after the publication of *A Sentimental Journey*, and she died ten years later, aged 34, by which time she had separated from her husband, enjoyed cult status as 'Sterne's Eliza', and was buried under a magnificent tomb. His corpse had no such rest; it was apparently stolen from the grave by body-snatchers and sold to Cambridge University, where in the middle of dissection class the great writer's physiognomy was recognised. This story may have more to do with Sterne's obsession with Yorick's skull in *Hamlet* than with actuality.

*[*Three famous love affairs; Paul Scarron (1610–1660), French dramatist, poet, invalid and opium addict, married Madame de Maintenon, 25 years younger than him; Edmund Waller (1606–87), poet and politician, wrote poems to Lady Dorothy Sidney 'Sacharissa'.]*

Portrait (detail) by Richard Cosway. Private collection. Photograph used with permission of The Laurence Sterne Trust.

Richard Brinsley Sheridan and Lady Harriet Duncannon

The 41-year-old playwright, theatre owner and Whig member of parliament is writing in anguish to his 30-year-old lover, Lady Harriet Duncannon, about the grave illness of his wife, Eliza, caused in part by his philandering. The impetuous Sheridan had eloped with Eliza Linley in 1772 when he was 20 and she a famous teenage singer. Eliza put up with his dedicating his greatest play, *The School for Scandal*, to a lover, Mrs Crewe, but his affair with the exciting Lady Harriet destroyed their marriage. (Harriet was a Spencer, sister of the notorious Georgiana, Duchess of Devonshire, mother of Lord Byron's histrionic lover Lady Caroline Lamb, and ancestor of Diana, Princess of Wales.) Eliza, lonely and depressed, started an affair with the dashing United Irishman, Lord Edward Fitzgerald. (Yes, it's all beginning to read like an 18th-century *Heat* magazine.) At the time of this letter, Eliza was ill and heavily pregnant with Fitzgerald's child. Though addressed to Harriet, this is Sheridan's love letter to Eliza, and is a melancholy reverie on the passage of time, similar in setting and sentiment to Matthew Arnold's 'Dover Beach', written half a century later. Parts of this letter were obliterated, probably by Harriet.

Richard Sheridan, engraving.

[SOUTHAMPTON]
Tuesday Night [Mar. 1792]

I wrote to you in rather good spirits yesterday … [obliterated] for I like the Quiet of this spot and E. seem'd much better and I wrote in the morning when the gloom upon everyone's mind is lighter. But now I am just returned from a long solitary walk on the beach. Night Silence Solitude and the Sea combined will unhinge the cheerfulness of anyone, where there has been length of Life enough to bring regret in reflecting on many past scenes, and to offer slender hope in anticipating the future… [three lines obliterated].

There never has been any part of your letters that have won my attention and interested me so much as when you have appeared earnestly solicitous to convey to my mind the Faith the Hope and the Religious Confidence which I do believe exist in yours. Accomplish this … if you can – and if there is any true merit in convincing selfish incredulity, or reclaiming those who tho' not quite hardened, can find no solace in seeking for truths they must dread … [erasures]

How many years have pass'd since on these unceasing restless waters which this Night I have been gazing at and listening to, I bore poor E. who is now so near me fading in sickness from all her natural attachments and affections, and then loved her so that had she died as I once thought she would in the Passage I should have assuredly plunged with her body to the Grave. What times and what changes have passed! You … [erasures] what have been, what are your sufferings? what has the interval of my Life been, and what is left me – but misery from Memory and a horror of Ref[l]exion? –

Eliza gave birth to a daughter, Mary, soon after this letter but died a few months later. Sheridan remained friends with Lord Edward, accepted Mary as his child, and was devastated when she died before she was two.

Sheridan and Esther Jane Ogle

In 1795 he married Esther Jane Ogle, the vivacious 19-year-old daughter of the Dean of Winchester. A besotted husband, he wrote her often and lovingly (calling her 'Hecca' and himself 'Dan') but remained subject to depression. The following letter, written four years into their marriage, is markedly similar to the earlier letter: again he is walking a familiar spot, thinking of the past. Although his circumstances and memories are happier than on the previous occasion when Eliza lay dying, the mere act of recollection produces the same melancholy effect. However, within two days he has cheered up – or at least he remembers to tell her how much he loves her, and to bless their baby son.

[24–27 Mar. 1799]

BEDFONT. SUNDAY EVENING.

Here am I, my Beloved Hecca, at my little Inn after writing all the rainy Part of the morning and walking seven miles on the Heath during two fine hours from five to seven – and then our Dinner. After I parted from you yesterday my Soul's Love I never felt more oppress'd and out of Heart. Bab walk'd with me a good way on the road we talk'd of Hecca and time back – which I could not avoid doing altho' it was the recollection of Time past that had me nervous, yet with no reflexions accompanying that recollection but such as ought to have made me cheerful. –

It was more than four years and four months since I had first talk'd to her of Hecca – before dear Hecca was mine – in that very walk, and assuredly I have now on proof a thousand times stronger ground to build my happiness upon, and upon experience, than Hope and Presumption could then have held out for me. Yet the memory of the past day was oppressive to my mind. The Truth is that the Death of Time and the recollection of departed Hours, if happily spent never can be chearful recollections. And if there is added to that the regret that those hours have not been prized enough, or all the happiness attach'd to them which might have been, the reviewing them and reflecting on them is still more painful. –

London. Tuesday Night. My own Wench – Dan left off writing to you on Sunday in a melancholy mood and He did not even say that which was uppermost in his mind that He loves you more and more a thousand times than ever and you shall see there shall be [an] end of the least cause of Hecca's fretting. I staid [?] so long at Bedfont yesterday working like a Team of Horses that I was not in Town in Time for the Post – and to Day with my usual ill management I left my Papers at home meaning to come in before Dinner and finish my Letter, but business kept me out the whole Day so that I shall be in high Disgrace with my own good Hecca who does not neglect Dan but writes like a dear good Girl. I really have done more business as well as Rolla than you could imagine. Tomorrow I will fix to an hour my seeing you and we will undoubtedly make a short visit to Knoyle and tell John [Ogle] I will really bring him some Plans. Bless you my Heart's Love I hope for a Line again tomorrow tho' I have been so bad – bless my Boy [their son, Robin].

Wednesday […] I will be with you on Saturday to Dinner, if not by your own green eyes on Sunday.

Heaven thee bless and guard S

Indeed Sukey, I would have come sooner but it has been physically impossible.

[The Letters of Richard Brinsley Sheridan, *edited by Cecil Price (Oxford University Press, 1966).*]

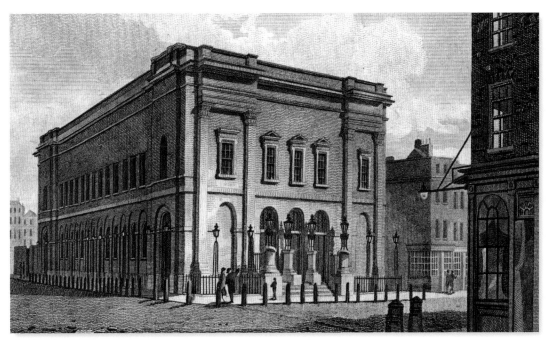

New Drury Lane Theatre

Sheridan's end was as melancholy as his mood in these letters: in 1809 his Drury Lane theatre burnt down; in 1812 he lost his seat in parliament; in 1814 and 1815 he was imprisoned for debt; and in 1816 he died in poverty. Meanwhile his wife had stashed away a fortune, £40,000, for their son.

Theobald Wolfe Tone and Matilda Tone

Wolfe Tone silk cigarette card

In France on revolutionary business, Theobald Wolfe Tone (32) writes his wife, Matilda (27), the kind of letters most wives would like to receive: loving, affectionate, jocular, high-spirited, concerned for her health, frank and confiding about his plans and the danger he faces. He signs with his *nom de guerre*, J[ames] Smith. His mood is remarkably buoyant considering he is writing only six weeks after the failure of his long-planned invasion (the French fleet bound for Ireland scattered due to bad weather and the few ships that reached Bantry Bay could not disembark). In the addendum, addressed to his small daughter, Tone is still making jokes to amuse Matilda. They were almost twelve years married; she had eloped with him in July 1785, a month before her sixteenth birthday and his twenty-second. His salute here – 'You do not know, you ugly thing, how much I love you' – is among the most affectionate oxymorons in the history of love letters.

11th February, 1797

My dearest Life and Soul,

Your letter of the 26th of last month has taken a mountain off my breast. I hope and trust you are daily getting better, and that the terrible apprehensions which I have been under since the receipt of your first will be belied by the event. You do not know, you ugly thing, how much I love you. I hope you are by this time, settled somewhere near Hamburgh where you may live at less expense than you can in the city, and with more comfort; live with the greatest economy, unless where your health is concerned, and in that case spare nothing. In one word, take the greatest

The Destruction of the French Armada — a contemporary cartoon by James Gillray.

possible care of yourself for ten thousand reasons, one of which is that if anything were to happen to you I could not, I think, live without you. When I have lately been forced once or twice to contemplate that most terrible of all events, you cannot imagine to yourself what a dreary wilderness the world appeared to me, and how helpless and desolate I seemed to myself. But let us quit this dispiriting subject and turn to another more encouraging.

I gave you in my last a short sketch of our unlucky expedition, for the failure of which we are, ultimately, to blame the winds alone, for as to an enemy we saw none. In the event, the British took but one frigate and two or three transports, so you see the rhodomantades [bragging] which you read in the English papers were utterly false. […] *General Hoche*, who commanded our expedition in chief has, it seems, taken a liking to me, for this very blessed day he caused to be signified to me that he thought of taking me, in his family, to the Army of *Sambre and Meuse,* which he is appointed to command, to which I replied, as in duty bound, that I was at all times ready to obey his orders; so, I fancy, go I shall. I did not calculate for a campaign on the Rhine, though I was prepared for one on the Shannon; however, my honour is now engaged and, therefore (sings),

> Were the whole army lost in smoke,
> Were these the last words that I spoke.
> I swear (and damn me if I joke)
> I had rather be with you.

If I go, as I believe I shall, you may be very sure that I will take all care of myself that may be consistent with my duty, and besides, as I shall be in the General's family, and immediately attached to his person, I shall be less exposed; and finally *'dost thou think that Hawser Trunnion, who has stood the fire of so many floating batteries, runs any risk from the lousy pops of a landsman?'*.* I rely upon your courage in this, as on every former occasion in our lives; our situation is today a thousand times more desirable than when I left you in Princeton; between ourselves I think I have not done badly since my arrival in France; and so you will say when you read my memorandums. I came here, knowing not a single soul, and scarcely a word of the language; I have had the good fortune, thus far, to obtain the confidence of the Government, so far as was necessary for our affair, and to secure the good opinion of my superior officer, as appears by the station I hold. It is not every stranger who comes into France and is made Adjutant-General 'with *two* points on his shoulder' as you say right enough; but that is nothing I hope to what is to come (sings) *'Zounds, I will soon be a Brigadier.'*

If I join the army of the Sambre and Meuse I shall be nearer to you than I am here, and we can correspond, so in that respect we lose nothing; and as my lot is cast in the army I must learn a little of the business, because *I am not at all without very well founded expectation* that we may have occasion to display our military talents elsewhere; in the meantime, I am in the best school and under one of the best masters in Europe. I cannot explain myself further to you by letter; remember the motto of our arms, 'never despair!' and as I see as little, and *infinitely less reason* to despair this day, than I did six months after my arrival in France so (sings) *'Madame you know my trade is war!'* I think this is a very musical letter.

[...]

As I shall remain, at all events, for a few days at Paris, I will write to you once or twice more before my departure. I must take up the remainder of this with a line to a young lady of my acquaintance, who has done me the honour to begin a correspondence with me.

Your ever-affectionate husband,
J.S. Adjt. Gen.!! Huzza, huzza!

Quotation from Tobias Smollett's The Adventures of Peregrine Pickle.

Dearest Baby [his daughter Maria],

You are a darling little thing for writing to me, and I doat upon you, and when I read your pretty letter, it brought the tears into my eyes, I was so glad. I am delighted with the account you give me of your brothers: […] I am not surprised that Frank is a bully, and I suppose he and I will have fifty battles when we meet. Has he got into a jacket and trousers yet? Tell your Mamma, from me, *'we do defer it most shamefully, Mr Shandy* [from Laurence Sterne's, *Tristram Shandy*]. I hope you take great care of your poor Mamma, who, I am afraid, is not well; but I do not need to say that, for I am sure you do, because you are a darling good child, and I love you more than all the world. Kiss your Mamma, and your two little brothers, for me, ten thousand times, and love me, as you promise, as long as you live.

Your affectionate Fadoff

J. SMITH

Eighteen months later, Tone sailed to Ireland with the second ill-fated French fleet, which was hastily assembled to buttress the 1798 rebellion. Captured in Buncrana, he was condemned to death by hanging, but slit his throat in prison, taking a few days to die. Matilda lived in France on a State pension until the Napoleonic defeat in 1815, then remarried, and moved to New York. With her only surviving child, William, she published Tone's marvellous autobiography and diaries in 1826, thus immortalising him. Like his siblings, William succumbed to tuberculosis, dying in 1828. Matilda lived on until 1849.

[The Letters of Wolfe Tone, *edited Bulmer Hobson.*]

Daniel O'Connell and Mary O'Connell

Mary O'Connell and her youngest son Daniel, by Gubbins, (detail) Derrynane House, Killarney.

The brilliant young Kerry barrister and future 'Liberator', Daniel O'Connell (26), is writing one of his ardent love letters to his distant cousin, Mary O'Connell (23), to whom he is secretly engaged. Because she was dowry-less, they feared his uncle Hunting Cap's rage if they married. O'Connell wrote often and lovingly from assizes, but this letter is uncharacteristically miserable and frantic; to punish him for the 'offence' of not writing her by every post, Mary had written him a 'ceremonious' letter, beginning 'Dear Sir' and ending 'your affectionate cousin'. She regarded it as a joke but he was appalled by the 'cold', 'sentimental', 'saucy' character she revealed in that letter and takes this opportunity to point out the sweet, modest virtues he loves in his 'little woman'.

9 February 1802

You see you were mistaken, my dearest love, I did not laugh at your former letter to me. Indeed, its producing a comical effect on me would be directly contrary to every impression I entertain of you. I trust and am pretty confident that this experiment will suffice and that you will not in future sport with the feelings which you know are too sensitive to bear being played on.

Daniel O'Connell

How could you, my only darling, treat me so coldly on so slight an occasion for you had not insisted that I should write to you by every post. And surely, surely, my dearest girl, you did know that your affections, your regard, were dearer to me than anything else in the world. I have told you I was proud of your love … Judge then how mortified I felt at finding so small an offence – shall I call it an offence? – put every idea of tenderness out of your bosom. For affection you could substitute thus easily the cold language of sentiment … Do, I entreat you, look upon even the pain which your ceremonious letter gave me as a decisive proof of the energy of my affection …Let me therefore anxiously and earnestly entreat that you will not use me in the same slighting manner in future. I beg of you, my love, humbly but as a favour which I think my respectful regard for you merits, that you will consider seriously before you treat me with such coldness. Indeed, indeed, I am unable to bear it. Could I tell you the pleasure your letter of the third gave me I should certainly do more than has yet been done in language of any kind … I again found you what you are, what you ever must always be, my own dear little woman. You cannot conceive how the character becomes you in my eyes. You look a thousand times handsomer and better in my eyes as my little woman than as my affectionate cousin. That affectionate cousin is a saucy little baggage. I beg you not to keep her company. On the contrary, I entreat you will avoid her entirely. As for my little woman it is impossible for anyone to meet with by an hundred degrees so sweet, so amiable, so interesting, so sensible and so charming a little girl. In disposition and heart she is all excellence, in temper all sweetness, in person all that painting can express or youthful poets fancy when they love. To tell you how much I love my little woman would be to express that of which no image can be formed. Think how much you love me and then add hundred thousand times as much and you will still have a feeble idea of the measure of my affection.

Love to your mother etc. How I long to press you to the heart of

Your fond husband
Daniel O'Connell

Though married secretly five months later, on the 24th of July 1802, they continued to live apart and Hunting Cap was not informed of the wedding for six months. When he heard, he (in O'Connell's words), 'got into a most violent flood of tears' and was 'more grieved and exasperated than we were aware of'. The tension made Mary ill. O'Connell wrote anxiously, ordering her to rally. She replied with this typically calm, loving and spirited letter, which in time-honoured fashion seeks to shield the star-cross'd lovers from an envious, gossiping, materialistic world.

[Postmarked Tralee] 6 February 1803

It will, I am pretty sure, give my dearest darling pleasure to hear his Mary is so much recovered as to be able to receive visitors all this day … It was uneasiness and grief that brought this last illness on me, grief, my darling, at parting with you and uneasiness lest your uncle's displeasure should affect you too much. It is not his fortune, I know, you would regret losing, but incurring the displeasure of an uncle whom I so well know you felt a sincere love for, gave me more unhappiness than I can describe. However, I trust before many months elapse, he will be reconciled to you. Should he not, my darling, at all events he can't prevent us from being happy together. I declare to you most solemnly that if he altered his will tomorrow it would not give me a moment's unhappiness. It was not your fortune but yourself, my dearest heart, that I married. If you were possessed of but fifty pounds a year, I would be happy with you and think myself one of the most enviable women in the world, blessed with such a fond adoring husband. May God, my darling, preserve you to your Mary. You would laugh a good deal were you here, love, [to hear] the various reports that are set forward every day. One of them is that your mother is so

Daniel O'Connell by Bernard Mulrenin, watercolour and bodycolour on ivory, 1836 © National Portrait Gallery, London.

exasperated that she never got out of bed since John [O'Connell's brother] went home. I listen to those stories and am quite indifferent about what they say or can say as I know it all proceeds from envy. What astonished them most, they exclaim, is my seeming indifference at your being disinherited by your uncle for so they will have it, because they would wish it … I do not give way to any grief at the displeasure of your uncle. Rick Connell is here and will not let me write more and, as he is a doctor, I must submit …

As a newly-wed, she may have been ready to marry on fifty pounds a year, but as the mother of a large family she was made increasingly unhappy by O'Connell's financial recklessness, which left them often on the verge of bankruptcy. The rumours of his philandering must also have upset her although she never referred to them in letters. Nevertheless, their marriage was long and loving, and their letters grew more, not less, affectionate. O'Connell was heartbroken by her death in 1836, and survived her by less than a decade.

[The Correspondence of Daniel O'Connell, Vol I, 1792–1814, *edited by Maurice R. O'Connell, 1973.*]

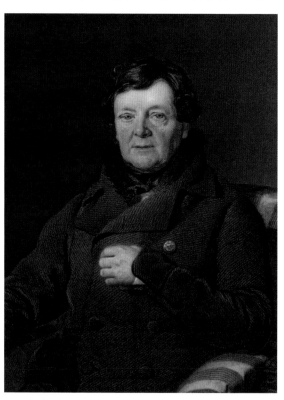

Daniel O'Connell, engraving by W. Hall.

Robert Emmet and Sarah Curran

Robert Emmet silk cigarette card

This nervous, witty letter from Sarah Curran to Robert Emmet is undated and unsigned, but since it refers to him in hiding, was almost certainly written in August 1803. Emmet's rebellion has failed; he is hiding out in Harold's Cross, and his housekeeper, Anne Devlin, is acting as the lovers' courier. Lovers enjoy secrecy but there was nothing melodramatic about Emmet and Curran's precautions. She was the 21-year-old daughter of John Philpot Curran, radical barrister, MP of genius and a domestic tyrant. Emmet, four years older, was a brilliant former Trinity student and debater for whom a great future had been predicted. If his hiding place were discovered, he faced death. If their affair were discovered, Sarah faced conspiracy charges and, worse, her father's fury. Fear keeps bursting through the surface of this letter, which still manages to be witty. She doesn't hide her nervous disposition – the result of growing up in the fraught Curran household – but also displays the spirit and subtle humour which drew Emmet. By the end she has written herself round to better form but doesn't forget to repeat an earlier request: burn this letter.

Sarah Curran by George Romney

[undated, c. August 1803]
[PRIORY, RATHFARNHAM]

I have been intending these many days past to write you a few lines, but was really incapable of conveying anything like consolation and altho' I felt that there might have been a momentary gratification in hearing from me, I feared that the communication of my feeling would only serve to irritate and embitter your own. Besides this, I felt a degree of reluctance in writing which, after what has passed may be rather inconsistent, but which is increased by considering the extent of the risque [risk] I run, as well as by the breach of propriety it occasions.

[…] I am afraid you heard no very gratifying account by the last express of my health and spirits. I was so certain of hearing from you early in the day, as she [Anne Devlin] had promised, that I concluded the poor greyhound was lost, or, still worse, might have been found. Altho' I may laugh now, I assure you I feared the worst, and was never more unhappy. I shall never forget the sensation of agony I felt while reading your letter. I assure you that my head suddenly felt as if it was burning and for a few minutes I think I was in fever. As for your letter, I did not understand it at the time, and had only a confused idea that you must leave the country for ever, as your mother wished it. You must therefore attribute to mental derangement my wish of seeing you at present. Do not think it, unless it might be done with safety, which I think impossible. At any rate, in the present circumstances, is it not wiser to limit myself to the gratification of knowing you are well and safe?

I should wish particularly to know from you how matters stand at present (if you would not be afraid); particularly what are your hopes from abroad and what you think they mean to do, and whether if they pay us a visit we shall not be worse off than before. […]

I had almost forgot to mention the letter I so officiously wrote to inform you of the honour intended your country residence [Emmet's previous hiding place in Wicklow] by his Majesty's troops, which I suspected the day before it happened; and having with my usual sapience written the letter and mentioned in the outside cover the number of our house and name of street for fear of any mistake, I only waited for an ambassador, when unfortunately for Homer he presented himself and was unlucky enough to be trusted. As he approached the bridge, seeing what was going forward, – about nineteen people whose pockets were searching – he committed his precious deposit to his boot, and marched up to the gate like another Achilles, vulnerable only in the heel. His pockets were soon turned inside out, where, to use an elegant phrase, the devil might have danced a hornpipe without kicking his shins against a half-penny. His Horace [presumably a book] was taken for the inspection of Government, and he was sent back in disgrace.

[…] You ought to be obliged to me for making you laugh – *malgre vous*. I believe you will find out that I began and ended this letter in very different moods. I began it in the morning, and it is now near two o'clock at night. I passed the house you are in twice this day, and did not see you. If I thought you were in safety I would be comparatively happy, at least. I cannot help listening to every idle report; and

Sarah Curran Playing the Harp
by William Beechey 1805, Calderdale
MBC Museums and Galleries.

although I cannot suppose that the minute events which occur now can materially influence the grand and general effect in view, yet my mind is risen or depressed as I suppose them favourable or otherwise. I cannot tell you how uneasy I shall be until I know if you have got this. Let me know immediately. I request you to burn it instantly. I shall expect a letter from you to tell me if you are well and in spirits. Try and forget the past, and fancy that everything is to be attempted for the first time. I long to know how your wife and ten small children are. Goodbye, my dear friend, but not for ever. Again I bid you burn this.

John Philpot Curran by unknown artist, oil on canvas, circa 1807
© *National Portrait Gallery, London.*

Emmet didn't burn it 'instantly' – but then she also failed to burn his letters – so that when he was captured on the 25th of August, this and another letter were found on him. The authorities, missing the obvious sincerity of the emotion, decided the letters were code from a fellow conspirator – they took the 'ten small children' (presumably a joking projection to their married future) to refer to ten army depots. Having adopted a cavalier attitude to interrogation, Emmet fell to pieces when the letters were produced and offered to plead guilty if they were suppressed. This was refused. After securing John Philpot Curran as his counsel, he wrote a quick note to Sarah, explaining the capture of her letters but reassuring that her name is safe. It is panicked, and not a love letter until the end:

Destroy my letters that there may be nothing against yourself, and deny having any knowledge of me further than seeing me once or twice. For God's sake, write to me by the bearer one line to tell me you are in spirits. I have no anxiety, no care, about myself; but I am terribly oppressed about you. My dearest love, I would with joy lay down my life, but ought I to do more? Do not be alarmed; they may try to frighten you, but they cannot do more. God bless you my dearest love.

    I must send this off at once; I have written it in the dark. My dearest Sarah, forgive me.

It was unwise to close with her name, and he then made the fatal error of entrusting the letter to a prison guard he trusted, who instead brought it to the Chief Secretary. Two days later the Curran household was searched; Sarah had convulsions but her sister, Amelia, had the presence of mind to burn Emmet's letters. An incensed John Philpot now refused to act as Emmet's counsel and forced Sarah out of the family home (though it was only his prominence that saved her from conspiracy charges). In his last days, Emmet wrote of his feelings for Sarah in a letter to her brother, which may be considered his valedictory love letter. The last lines reinforce our image of Sarah as fragile and in need of a prop to cling to.

[c.18th September 1803]

I intended as much happiness for Sarah as the most ardent love could have given her. I never did tell you how much I idolised her. It was not with a wild or unfounded passion, but it was an attachment increasing every hour, from an admiration of the purity of her mind and respect for her talents. I did dwell in secret upon our union. [...] I did not look for honours for myself – praise I would have asked from the lips of no man; but I would have wished to read in the glow of Sarah's countenance that her husband was respected.

 My love, Sarah! It was not thus that I thought to have requited your affection. I did hope to be a prop round which your affections might have clung, and which would never have been shaken; but a rude blast has snapped it, and they have fallen over a grave.

Her affections may have fallen over a grave, but not one she had the consolation of visiting. After Emmet's execution by hanging on the 20th of September 1803, his body was hidden to prevent his grave becoming a rallying point. Two years later Sarah married an army officer who treated her well, but she suffered depression and poor health, and, soon after the death of her infant son, she died on the 3rd of May 1808. Her father refused her final wish to be buried at the family home beside a sister who died in childhood.

The execution of Robert Emmet.

Mary Ann McCracken and Thomas Russell

The 33-year-old radical Belfast Presbyterian, Mary Ann McCracken, is writing to the condemned United Irishman, Thomas Russell (36), in Downpatrick Gaol, where he is awaiting execution for his part in Robert Emmet's rebellion. It is a ghastly re-enactment of the execution five years earlier, after the 1798 rebellion, of Henry Joy McCracken, Mary Ann's favourite brother and Russell's best friend. In later life, Mary Ann described the handsome, charismatic and promiscuous Russell in aching terms, 'A model of manly beauty, he was one of those favoured individuals whom one cannot pass in the street without being guilty of the rudeness of staring in his face when passing'. However, he seems to have regarded her only as a friend. There is no conclusive proof that she was in love with him, but this poignant hesitant letter seems tense with things unsaid. After begging in convoluted language to let her know how she can help any who 'have claims on his affection' she finally cracks and pleads for a lock of his hair, before quickly retreating to apologies for imposing on him.

[October 1803]

I hoped to have had the pleasure of seeing you once more but as that satisfaction seems now improbable I feel most deeply at the disappointment, not that I supposed your mind required the support of any human consolation, possessing as you do that comfort which the world can neither give nor take away — but I wished to have assured you of my intentions of continual friendship to your sister & also to request if there are any others who have claims on your affection, that you will not thro' motives of false delicacy scruple to mention them [,] that those who shall ever venerate your memory may know how to show it that respect of which it is so truly deserving — it is impious and certainly cruel in us to repine at the prospect of your removal from a world every way so unworthy of you, yet it is impossible to divest

The United Irish Patriots of 1798 (Samuel Neilson; Michael Dwyer; John Sheares; William Corbet; Arthur O'Connor; Archibald Hamilton Rowan; William Jackson; William James Macneven (Macnevin); Matthew Teeling; Robert Emmet; Henry Sheares; Theobald Wolfe Tone; James Napper Tandy; Thomas Addis Emmet; James Hope; Henry Joy MacCracken; Thomas Russell; Lord Edward Fitzgerald) after unknown artist, coloured lithograph, 1798 or after © National Portrait Gallery, London.

oneself so entirely of selfishness as not to feel the deepest regret for the loss society will sustain in being deprived of one of its most valuable members – a firm reliance on the wisdom and goodness of that Providence that governs the universe & who does not permit afflictions in vain, can alone reconcile us to such a melancholy event – if there is anything I can do either now or hereafter that would in the least degree contribute to your satisfaction you cannot gratify me more highly than by naming your wishes – I have no doubt but that one day will arrive when your loss & such as yours will be universally deplored even by those who are at present more active against you. May I request that you will indulge me with another lock of your hair, that I received already & for wh[ich] I am particularly obliged I had to divide with my sister & my friend Eliza, each of us shall preserve our [torn] invaluable treasure as a memento of virtue seldom equalled & worthy of affection [torn] of imitation. Forgive me for imposing so long on your so very precious time, [torn] to be considered worthy of your friendship is an honour which we shall ever most highly value. I am joined by my sister in every sentiment of attachment & veneration.

I remain,
Yours most truly,
M. McC

She need not have worried about imposing, and could have written what she wished – her letter was handed to Russell the morning of his execution but he did not read it 'lest it disturbed his mind'. Mary Ann never married, but lived a long, useful life in Belfast, campaigning for women's rights, the abolition of slavery and numerous other causes until her death at 96.

[Mary McNeill, The Life and Times of Mary Ann McCracken, 1770–1886, a Belfast panorama (The Blackstaff Press, 1960).]

Hector Berlioz and Harriet Smithson

The febrile young French composer, Hector Berlioz (28) is writing to his muse, the Irish actress Harriet Smithson, who is five years older. It is an overwrought, hysterical letter, but then the circumstances are remarkable: after stalking her for five years and writing masterpieces for her, he is about to meet her for the first time (or they have just met). Harriet, born and raised in Ennis,

was not critically acclaimed, but was exquisitely beautiful. Her looks and fervid temperament suited Shakespeare's *ingénue* parts, and it was as Ophelia that Berlioz saw her in Paris on the 11th of September 1797 in a performance that earned her the title 'La Belle Irlandaise'. The effect on him was cataclysmic: he became obsessed with Shakespeare, was inspired to write the 'Mélodie Irlandaise' and 'Symphonie fantastique', and began following her around Paris, even taking rooms opposite her apartment. Smithson, warned that he was epileptic and unstable, ignored him until she heard the 'Fantastique' performed on the 9th of December 1832. As her biographer writes, 'It is not everyone who is wooed by a full orchestra'; she sent him congratulations. This letter, which masochistically blesses the suffering she's caused him, was written either just before or just after their first meeting.

[Paris, between 10 and 18 December 1832]

A Mademoiselle Henriette Smithson,
RUE DE RIVOLI, HOTEL DE CONGRÈS

Si vous voulez pas ma mort, au nom de la pitié, (je n'ose dire de l'amour), faites-moi savoir quand je pourrai vous voir. Je vous demande grâce, pardon à genoux, avec sanglots!!!

Oh! malheureux que je suis, je n'ai pas cru mériter tout ce que je souffre, mais je bénis les coups qui viennent de votre main.

J'attends votre réponse comme l'arrêt de mon juge.

H. Berlioz

[If you don't wish for my death, in the name of pity (I dare not say of love), let me know when I can see you. I beg you for mercy, and ask sobbing on my knees for forgiveness!!!

Oh! Wretch that I am, I didn't believe I deserved all that I suffered, but I bless the blows that come from your hand.

I await your reply like the sentence from a judge.]

The rest of their operatic relationship is told in his letters to others. One week later he wrote to his friend, the composer Franz Liszt:

Everything about her delights and exalts me; the frank confession of her feelings has astounded me and driven me almost mad. […] I will never leave her. She is my star. She has understood me. If it is a mistake, you must allow me to make it; she will adorn the closing days of my life, which, I hope will not last long. […]Yes, I love her! I love her! And I am loved. She told me that herself yesterday in front of her sister; yes she loves me, […] but I wish to keep my happiness secret if it is possible. So, silence!

Franz Liszt

She tentatively agreed to marry him, but their families were against the match, and 'she trembles, she hesitates, and does not know how to make up her mind: however will all this end?' He forced the issue by poisoning himself in front of her:

> Frightful shrieks from Henriette [Harriet], sublime despair, cruel laughter on my part, desire to live again on witnessing her protestations of love! An emetic! Ipecacuana! Vomiting for two hours …Only two grains of opium left; I was ill for three days and recovered. Henriette, in despair and seeking to make up for what she's done to me, asked what I wanted her to do.

They were married on the 3rd of October 1833. Things quickly turned sour; he took lovers and she took to drink; they separated within ten years. After a bizarre incident in which a mysterious gunman shot at her, she had the first of five strokes, which paralysed her, and died on the 3rd of March 1854. Liszt wrote her a cold epitaph which stands for many muses: 'She inspired you, you loved her, you sang of her, her task was done'.

Hector Berlioz

Annie Hutton and Thomas Davis

Twenty-year-old Annie Hutton, writing to Thomas Davis, seems even more delirious than most fiancées. The daughter of a wealthy Dublin Protestant merchant, she had fallen in love with the journalist, balladeer and Young Irelander on first sight when she was eighteen, but her parents were against the match because of Davis' association with Daniel O'Connell, then seeking repeal of the Union. By August 1845 her mother at least had come round, perhaps because of Davis' estrangement from O'Connell, and the pair got engaged. The handsome thirty-year-old Davis was already nationally famous as founder and main contributor to the massively popular weekly, *The Nation*, and Annie's attitude seems a little star-struck; she thinks him 'more noble and good' than her 'self-willed, passionate, vain' self, but she was spirited, humorous and intelligent and at the end of the letter delivers a scathing attack on what she sees as his elitist contempt for his readers.

Thursday, 12 o'clock
[August 1845]

Dearest friend, I fear you must have thought me sadly cold yesterday, but indeed I could not have said a word. My happiness was too great, my love too deep for utterance, but I thought you were disappointed that I did not tell you so. It was like a dream of joy too beautiful to be realised, and I can hardly believe it yet. And then this morning on awaking there was your dear kind letter, ah! How I thank you for it. No, you did not agitate me yesterday, & do you think you could weary me? Don't say that again dearest, & wont you come early on Sunday, really early, not five o'clock, for I have so much to say to you; perhaps when you know me better, you will not love me so much, for you do not know half my faults, how self-willed, how passionate, how vain I am. And I want you to promise me one thing, that whenever you see or hear anything you don't like, won't you tell me directly, for I have perfect confidence in you, you are everything that is noble and good. Oh I am very happy, a happiness above all I ever dreamt of. Is not my precious Mammie good to us, we can never tell her how much we owe to her, how much we love her. She showed me all your letters, and gave me back all my poetry; that sad Sunday that your first letter came & she thought I must give you up, I gave her all you had ever given me, & in the bitterness of my grief, wondered if ever I should be happy again as I was before. Ah we did not think of yesterday.

You need not have been jealous of poor little Nizza [a pet?], you know he died the next day, but I did not care. I cared for nothing, & was frightened at my own callousness. That was a long long week, – but I must not get sad – you have the sin on your conscience of my being late for breakfast this morning, for when Mammie gave me your letter somehow I wanted to read it, & then when I had read it, it wanted to be read again, & so, so I went on, reading & dreaming & being very happy. You must not write again for a long time, for I can't help thinking of you when the letters come (never at other times you know), & it is not good for me, when I can do nothing else, you know I shan't be fit to be your companion dearest, if I am ignorant & foolish. Do not write an answer to this, perhaps you never thought of it, but forgive my vanity, now I really mean what I say, for I am not one of those young ladies who say the contrary to what I mean, but come early on Sunday, & we will have a long talk. Yes I will tell you all I think and feel, not one thought shall be hid from you, my soul shall be yours as my heart is (i.e. nearly!) by & bye it will be all. This is a sadly selfish note, but won't you forgive me.

Why do you fear I shall change, have you less confidence in me than I in you, you will have more temptations, for all admire you. Thank you for the Aileen Aroon, but why do you say altered for the worse, is it because you put Annie instead of Aileen. Mind you write my name in the book of ballads, else I won't have it! I haven't quite forgiven yet your impertinent note, about being obliged to write gibberish, gibberish forsooth, & pretty looking stuff, to enable your common readers I suppose to understand you. My wrath is roused, the first time I read it I flung down the book in a rage, but afterwards picked it up again, & asked it to forgive. I could sit here writing for a long time, but must say goodbye to my dearest beloved friend, who has ever (nearly all) the love of his own Annie,

I am going to play Irish airs now, how I wish I could sing them.

These lovers were doomed; not because of parental opposition or politics, but because of poor health. In 1844 an ailing Annie had gone to Rome in search of sunshine, but it was Davis who died suddenly from scarlatina on the 16th of September 1845, just six weeks after their engagement, a month after this letter and at the start of the Great Famine. Annie wrote bravely to a friend of 'a short month of happiness … one short month, yet a whole existence of love'. She never married and eight years later died from an illness.

Charles Stewart Parnell and Katherine O'Shea

Charles Stewart Parnell (34), newly elected leader of the Irish home rule party and a busy man who neither opened nor answered his mail, is writing to Mrs Katherine O'Shea (35), wife of one of his supporters, Willie O'Shea, MP for Clare. As an aspiring political hostess, Mrs O'Shea had been trying for months to get Parnell's attention, sending him invitations to dinner. Finally she accosted him outside the House of Commons. This did the trick. He immediately sent her this letter, making a date for his return from Paris. He opens boldly with what is surely a pun on the Compensation for Disturbance Bill then going through parliament, and on his own 'disturbed' condition after meeting her. His reference to the 'powerful attractions' of Thomas's Hotel, where Mrs O'Shea was staying, is typically coy.

LONDON, July 17, 1880

MY DEAR MRS O'SHEA, – We have all been in such a 'disturbed' condition lately that I have been quite unable to wander further from here than a radius of about one hundred paces allons. And this notwithstanding the powerful attractions which have been tending to seduce me from my duty towards my country in the direction of Thomas's Hotel.

I am going over to Paris on Monday evening or Tuesday morning to attend my sister's wedding, and on my return will write you again and ask for an opportunity of seeing you. –

Yours very truly,
CHAS. S. PARNELL

She was equally smitten and they quickly embarked on an affair, meeting when they could in her home in Kent. By the autumn of 1881 she was pregnant with his child, and he was in prison for Land League agitation. These two notes were written on consecutive days immediately after his arrest in Morrison's Hotel, Dublin. They employ the baby-talk – 'Wifie', 'Queenie', 'brave little woman', 'your King' – that amused readers when Mrs O'Shea published his correspondence in a breathless biography in 1914. However, the postscript to the first note shows his other side: laconic, hard-nosed and politically savvy.

Willie O'Shea

MORRISON'S HOTEL, DUBLIN
October 13, 1881

MY OWN QUEENIE, – I have just been arrested by two fine-looking detectives, and write these words to wifie to tell her that she must be a brave little woman and not fret after her husband.

The only thing that makes me worried and unhappy is that it may hurt you and our child.

You know, darling, that on this account it will be wicked of you to grieve, as I can never have any other wife but you, and if anything happens to you I must die childless. Be good and brave, dear little wife, then.

YOUR OWN HUSBAND

Politically it is a fortunate thing for me that I have been arrested, as the movement is breaking fast, and all will be quiet in a few months, when I shall be released.

Parnell addressing The Irish Parliamentary Party.

[KILMAINHAM]
October 14, 1881

MY OWN DEAREST WIFIE, — I have found a means of communicating with you, and of your communicating in return.

Please put your letters into enclosed envelope, first putting them into an inner envelope, on the joining of which you can write your initials with a similar pencil to mine, and they will reach me all right.

I am very comfortable here, and have a beautiful room facing the sun – the best in the prison. There are three or four of the best of the men in adjoining rooms with whom I can associate all day long, so that time does not hang heavy nor do I feel lonely. My only fear is about my darling Queenie. I have been racked with torture all to-day, last night, and yesterday, lest the shock may have hurt you or our child. Oh darling, write or wire me as soon as you get this that you are well and will try not to be unhappy until you see your husband again. You may wire me here.

I have your beautiful face with me here; it is such a comfort. I kiss it every morning.

YOUR KING

Parnell may not be the most lyrical letter-writer, but he is among the most sincere. A reserved man, he seemed a confirmed bachelor by the time he met Mrs O'Shea, and without her may well 'have died childless'. As it was, the child she was carrying while he was in Kilmainham died two months after birth but they had two more daughters over the next few years. In December 1889, private rumour became public scandal when Captain O'Shea filed for divorce, citing Parnell as correspondent. The case famously split the Irish Parliamentary Party, destroyed Parnell's political career and hastened his early death. On the 25th of June 1891 'Queenie's darling King' was finally able to legally call her his 'dearest Wifie', but he died four months later. Among the correspondents included in this book only Emmet and Wilde paid as high and as public a price for love.

George Bernard Shaw and Alice Lockett

Twenty-seven-year-old George Bernard Shaw is using his considerable wit and insight to ensnare Alice Lockett, younger by a few years. He has no money or fame – theatrical success is still two decades away – but the middle-class, English, conventionally educated Alice is entranced and unsettled by the impecunious Irish bohemian. Throughout his long life Shaw carried on intense flirtations with numerous women, whom he bombarded with letters, but didn't generally seek to sleep with. He was a virgin until he was 29 and probably never consummated his marriage. This, his first surviving love letter, is fascinating for its insight into male desire in general, and his own mind in particular. Although he fell rapidly in love, he rarely suffered over it; here he admits that his heart is fundamentally cold, a 'machine'.

36 OSNABURGH STREET N W
9th September 1883

Forgive me. I don't know why, on my honor [sic]; but in playing on my own thoughts for the entertainment of the most charming of companions last night, I unskilfully struck a note that pained her – unless she greatly deceived me. I have felt remorseful ever since, and she has been reproaching herself all day for wilfully missing a train. Heavens! to regret having dared at last to be frank and kind! Did you not see at that moment a set of leading strings fall from you and hang themselves upon me in the form of golden chains? The heart of any other man would have stopped during those seconds after you had slowly turned your back upon the barrier and yet were still in doubt. Mine is a machine and did not stop; but it did something strange.

A playbill for Bernard Shaw's Captain Brassbound's Conversion.

It put me in suspense, which is the essence of woman's power over man, and which you had never made me feel before – I was always certain of what you would do until that question of the train arose. And I repaid you for the luxury by paining you. I did not intend to do so any more than you intended to please me, so forgive forgive forgive forgive forgive me.

I cannot (or perhaps will not) resist the impulse to write to you. Believe nothing that I say – I have a wicked tongue, a deadly pen, and a cold heart – I shall be angry with myself tomorrow for sending this, and yet, when I meet you, I shall plunge headlong into fresh cause for anger.

Farewell, dear Alice. There! Is it not outrageous? Burn it. Do not read it. Alas! It is too late: you have read it.

GBS

George Bernard Shaw

Drawing of Eliza Doolittle from Shaw's play Pygmalion.

Alice replied spiritedly and indignantly in a letter which is heavy on the insults; she is clearly palpitating.

11 September 1883

May I ask what was the object of your letter to me? Did you think it necessary to revive the pain caused by your words of last evening? All people are not machines: some are capable of genuine feelings. You know very well you have the power of paining me, and you are very careful in exercising it. You have done it over and over again. As I cannot accuse you of want of discrimination, I presume you enjoy the power you possess. Your letter proves what I have many times told you – that you are one of the weakest men I have ever met; and in spite of your cleverness I cannot help despising you. The warning not to trust you is a needless one: unless you have a very bad memory you will recall the fact of my having told you so often. Although you truly repudiated the idea of insincerity your letter is one of condemnation. Much more could I say, but I have said too much already.

She was no match for him. In his next letter he immediately pointed out the flaw in her reproaches – 'Come! If you meant all you said, you would not have written to me at all' – and proceeded to brilliantly contrast the conventional, forced, false side of her personality (which he calls 'Miss Lockett') with her real instinctive self, 'Alice'. Any woman would be fascinated and flattered by such close analysis from such a brilliant mind. The affair, like all his affairs, eventually petered out but, as always with him, they remained friends.

George Bernard Shaw

George Bernard Shaw and Mrs Campbell

Shaw married but went on with his amorous correspondences – he lavished epistolary affection on the actress Ellen Terry for five years, without meeting her – but the great passion of his life, for whom he was even willing to get physical, was the celebrated actress Mrs Patrick Campbell, who played Eliza Doolittle in the first production of his masterpiece, *Pygmalion*. For a year, 1912–13, the middle-aged lovers (he was 56 and she 47) indulged in a highly theatrical correspondence, termed by the editor of his letters, 'bravura performances by a virtuoso trifler and a notorious flirt'. Shaw was clearly writing with an eye on posterity, and Mrs Campbell

['Stella'], whose own literary style was more ramshackle, mocked him: *'How I detest letters written for an audience – in hopes of publication after death – Lord Chesterfield Madame de Sevigne Bernard Shaw – give me the impulsive, undated, unpunctuated, unreadable letters of a Campbell.'* In the following letter, she taunts him with the letters he might get if he weren't saving his correspondence for the British Museum, and with the sexual favours he might enjoy if he'd increase his virility by drinking beer and eating meat (he was a teetotaller vegetarian).

12 HINDE ST.

31st Jan. 1913

Hours for visitors from 12 a.m. to 11.30 p.m.

[…]

So you're no longer in love that means I may someday become a respected friend of the family, and who knows have cards left upon me! –

  •   No one can go to sleep at 11 AM it's ridiculous

What letters you would get if you didn't read 'bits aloud' and they were quickly put into the waste basket-

The British Museum indeed! how this trick of yours annoys me thinking everything pertaining to you will eventually find its way to the British Museum –
I adore and at the same time detest your fears and tremblings and bewitching timidities – 'late for dinner' 'not fit to work' unmanned 'if within a fortnight of a public appearance you shake the hand of a sick widow you professed to love! [e.g. herself]' – if only you'd eat red steaks and drink beer your spirit would be meet, I mean meet to mate – no I don't mean that –
What was that you said? 'Stella are you not afraid of sudden lightning' – and then you said something else – theres a deal to remember and cope with.

Stella

Mrs Campbell

What does she mean? Does she want to sleep with him or is she teasing? Shaw grew daily more infatuated, bombarding her with letters (one of which bested Stanley Kowalski by shouting 'Stella' twenty-nine times as an opening). The following letter is immensely stylish and artificial and reads, in its string of zany comparisons, like the Cole Porter song, 'You're the Tops'.

10 ADELPHI TERRACE W C
27th February 1913

Cruel stony hearted wretch, snatcher of bread from a starving child, how had you the heart? how could you? do you know what it means to me? I want my plaything that I am to throw away. I want my Virgin Mother enthroned in heaven. I want my Italian peasant woman. I want my rapscallionly fellow vagabond. I want my dark lady. I want my angel – I want my tempter. I want my Freia with her apples. I want the lighter of my seven lamps of beauty, honor [sic], laughter, music, love, life and immortality. I want my inspiration, my folly, my happiness, my divinity, my madness, my selfishness, my final sanity and sanctification, my transfiguration, my purification, my light across the sea, my palm across the desert, my garden of lovely flowers, my million nameless joys, my day's wage, my night's dream, my darling and my star. And you deny them all to me with six conventional words that do not even scorch the paper they are written on.

Very well: I will stay away, I will forget, I will drudge, I will do without, I will grind out articles and speeches amid the ruins of my temples & the fallen leaves of my trees. I will do my duty and relieve it with hideous laughter, joyless, hard, dead. Friday, Saturday, Sunday, Monday, not a moment, not a chance, not a possibility, four eternities:
O cruel, cruel, cruel, cruel, have you no heart at all?

GBS

But Mrs Campbell had moved on to a younger man. A thoroughly roused Shaw was finally galvanised into taking physical action. His attempts to seduce the now uninterested actress were farcical, as he recognised in a very funny letter (9th April 1913), which shows his ability to observe himself dispassionately.

Mrs Campbell

Have you ever dodged elusively round a room, with a weeping, howling, red faced, swollen, aged, distorted featured man pursuing you with a letter in his hand, pressing on you the documentary evidence in your own writing that you once loved or pretended to?

But it was his vanity rather than his heart that was damaged, as he admits in a flourish at the end of his entertainingly insulting valedictory letter (11th August): *'You have wounded my vanity: an inconceivable audacity, an unpardonable crime.'* She married the younger man, George Cornwallis-West, the following year; he deserted her six years later. She and Shaw continued to correspond warmly until her death in 1940, when she was 74 and he 83.

[Bernard Shaw, Collected Letters, *edited by Dan H. Laurence, 4 vols (Max Reinhardt, 1965–1988) and* Bernard Shaw and Mrs Patrick Campbell: Their Correspondence, *edited by Alan Dent (Victor Gollancz, 1952).]*

Alexander Crawford and Elizabeth Mathews

From a sheep station in the remote Australian outback, 27-year-old Alexander ('Alick') Crawford is writing to his fiancée and cousin, Elizabeth ('Lillie') Mathews, in Victoria, Australia. He has recently emigrated from Belfast; she emigrated as a child. Back in Belfast, Alexander's father opposed the marriage of cousins and was disappointed that his son was not following him into the family business; he either refused to give, or Alick refused to accept, money to ease his way in Australia. Stoical, practical and intense, Alick threw himself into work as manager of the station and poured love on Lillie in his frequent letters. His tone here is humorous, sometimes teasing and sensual, and lyrical in its use of refrains. His status as a recent emigrant, estranged from family and with few friends in the new country, undoubtedly strengthened his devotion.

19th-century Belfast

GERALDTON [WESTERN AUSTRALIA]
13 April 1882

I do hope I will be successful in this station. The last manager lost nearly £500 a year on it but everyone says it was through bad management. When I come to think of it it seems a risky undertaking for one with so little experience as myself to undertake to manage and bring a station, in a state of utter disorder, into good order. I have scarcely had one year's experience but if close attention to it and hard work will do anything towards making it I think it is not myself alone I am working for but for the dearest girl living. Oh Lillie my own true love I would undergo anything for your sweet sake and count it but pleasure if I but brought you the nearer to me. I often think what would life be to me now without the love of Lillie. I managed to get along in a kind of a way before but now it would be misery indeed. 'Tis the sweetest thought I have that before long I hope to take you to myself for better, there will be no worse in it. Sure there won't. Do tell me more about yourself in your letters, fill them up with Lillie, commence with Lillie, end with Lillie, and fill the space between with the same subject, and you may add a postscript about her too, it will not be too much. It is a subject I never weary reading about, writing about, or speaking about, so satisfy me in this respect my little girl. I am looking as if I had just escaped from prison, my hair cut close and my beard also. I do wish I could make my moustache grow a bit longer. It sticks at the one length much to my disgust. Is not this vanity worse than a girl, I fancy I can hear you say. Perhaps by the time you see me next it may have stretched a little and you may not be able to see my lips. How will that do?

Lillie was intelligent, humorous, principled and pious and replied in letters even more ardent and articulate than her fiancé's. In this masterly epistle, she begins sensuously, invoking their last kiss; moves onto spiritual love, and then uses her advantage – first placing herself metaphorically on his knee – to remind him of his religious duties. A devout Methodist, she worried greatly that there were no church services in the outback.

Emigrants readying for departure..

93

1880s Australian sheep station.

[LINTON, BALLARAT, VICTORIA]
27 July 1883

You ask me if I forget the 'loves' we used to have. I'll forget I am in existence as soon as forget that darling. How I dwell on the happy times we passed together and look forward to brighter and happier days. Nor do I forget the one [kiss] on the kitchen table. You remember it so vividly can you remember the first you gave me. I think it's time you blushed, please don't give the excuse that there is something red in the room. Dear me what an impudent cousin we had in those days. To think of the liberties he took, shocking!!! But I suppose you will be telling me we were just as naughty to permit such things. Ah well, perhaps we were. I remember the last kiss you gave me, the last real one in Aunt Mattie's parlour, you said 'we'll say goodbye now before any others come in' and we gave each other such a real love that it's fresh yet darling. I got another kiss after, but that was when we were all standing in the hall. Oh darling how vividly that day rises before me, how mechanically I went through every thing and tried to talk and laugh as usual, but Oh that I could have been alone, how I missed the one dear face so tenderly loved and the voice that thrilled through me. Your letters are all I could wish letters to be, but I miss the

Ballarat, 1880s

reality, the writer, a blank is here, which only you, darling, can fill. I want the loving substance, my heart craves for something that will not be satisfied without you. There's a continual unrest an eager expectation, a looking forward to hopes fulfilled, which will not be at rest till I feel I have you by me not to be separated. It's a very queer feeling, intense love for someone. It may be wrong, but I cannot help it that home does not satisfy me as it did a few years ago. I keep longing for something not in the home, a continual yearning to know how you are, whether you are well or not. But I do not wish you to think I am fretting darling, for I am not. I know how that would grieve you and do no good but perhaps harm. But you alone know the feelings I have and understand what the heart longs for and to you only would I thus write …

I have been going over your letter and now come to something I would like to speak to you about, but first try and think your little wife is on your knee with her arms round your neck and my head on your shoulder and you with your arm round my waist holding me to yourself and I tell you I want to say something and please give me your serious attention for a few minutes. It's this darling, in some places in your journal it grieved me to read that several times on Sunday you were out laying poisoned baits and riding some distance after sheep and one place firing at some birds in the garden. Now darling you may think I am making a fuss over very small things but darling may they not lead to larger things. I don't want to vex you but I do want my Alick to keep the Sabbath a holy day. These may be small things now, but unless you watch over yourself and pray, they may lead to larger inroads on the Sabbath. O my precious one, my own dear husband guard against the very appearance of evil. Your little girl prays for you darling and don't forget to pray for yourself my Alick. Don't neglect your study of God's word my own, do not neglect your precious soul's welfare, it needs daily nourishing and watering or it will go back and not forward. It is easy for me to write and advise easier far than to act I know, but darling it is for your good I write, but I love you very tenderly, you know this don't you, that I do not mean to be fault finding, but I write in love to you, *Alick my own.*

This touching correspondence ended in marriage on the 3rd of March 1885, five years after their first meeting. Lillie died six years later. Alick wrote to his brother that 'I have nothing to live for now no interest to work for', but eighteen months later he married Lillie's younger sister, Martha ('Mattie') Mathews; they had three children. After Mattie's death in 1921, he married, aged sixty-six, a much younger widow, Mrs Gladys Greenham; they had a son. Alick's best friend claimed this third marriage was one of the loveliest things he had ever known and Alick's son confirmed that 'a strange mixture of ages seemed to add to and not detract from the charm of their family life'. Alick was evidently uxorious.

[*Patrick O'Farrell*, Letters from Irish Australia 1825–1929 *(New South Wales University Press, 1984).*]

Families disembark at port in Autralia.

Edith Somerville and Martin Ross

23-year old Violet Martin is writing from her family estate, Castletownshend in Cork, to her distant cousin, Edith Somerville (28), who is in Paris studying art. They have only recently met and have not yet begun collaborating on their celebrated novels. The popular Somerville had many correspondents and was ignoring her shy cousin's letters, but Martin does not give up. This masterly letter of seduction, with its arresting opening – why should Somerville blush? – moves gracefully from teasing attack to devoted solicitude, managing *en route* – all in the spirit of wit and gossip – to get in an image of Martin draped in a tunic 'looking thoroughly indecent'. In the closing lines she seems to transpose her own feelings onto another of Somerville's admirers, the 'Commander', who 'loves you with reckless ardour' but 'can be a very good friend to his friends'. Or is 'the Commander' her name for herself?

Student at Colarossis Studio, Paris, pencil on paper, Crawford Art Gallery, Cork.
Edith Somerville, with her signature (above).

MALL HOUSE – CASTLET
May 19th '86

My dear Edith
You know and you should blush to know that there is no reason in the world why I should write to you – but there are people to whom it interests one to write irrespective of their bad qualities and behaviour – As I have heard each of your letters declaimed I have felt that I should like to make merry with you over many things

E.E. Somerville

The Goose Girl, Edith Somerville,
Crawford Art Gallery, Cork.

A Holy Place of Druids, oil on canvas, Edith Somerville., Crawford Art Gallery, Cork.

therein – but have been daunted by the thought of your many correspondents –You have one fatal fault – you are a 'popular girl' – a sort that I have always abhorred – so bear in mind that theoretically you are in the highest degree offensive to me. So you see that we are in our new house – I had a high old time over settling it while Mama was staying in Cork – and still have any amount to do – I have come to the conclusion that having to banish kamaks [knick-knacks] is better than the absolute death of them – The room here is so very unfurnished that I feel a fool when I sit down to read in it – It seems only a place to walk about in – However *respice ad finem* – if you were not such a popular girl I could say very nice things to you about your coming home – Seriously I shall be delighted to see you back again and so will everyone else – It is possible that I may meet you in London as I have an idea of going over to Kew about then for a fortnight – I have today had an invitation to Chatham there being a large ball on the 4th there with other delights – and I am tempted but somehow the Castle Townshend inertness has me in its grasp – It is so dreadful to think of getting clothes made – I am going up to Drishane this afternoon you will be surprised to hear, and will have a look at the Japanese garments before I send this off – so as to give you my valuable opinion but I am sure the blue is the one for you and the yellow for Hildegarde [Somerville's sister] – I wish you could have seen Hildegarde in her Japanese clothes at Harry's '*bal masque*' – she looked quite delicious – intensely Japanese – and yet handsome – If you can imagine the two things – Hers was a genuine good fancy dress [...] I daresay they told you that I went in a sheet draped *à la* greek statue – it looked thoroughly indecent, without being really so and was heaven in the way of comfort – I am sure if we all dressed like that we would be more ladylike and more agreeable – that dance was most pleasant and your mother has, I am confident, ideas of another at Drishane when you come back – I was grieved to hear that you had been sick and I daresay the sooner you leave Paris the better for you – You are an unhealthy though not a gross feeder (bar pancakes) and you ought to be looked after – What a good time you will have in London – and probably a good one at Walmer – Our Edith knows the latter place well – I see plainly that the Commander loves you with a reckless ardour – deny it if you can. I believe however he can be a very good friend to his friends.

[...]

Yours ever
Violet Martin

Somerville could not long withstand what she called her cousin's 'inveigling' and within nine months they had become regular correspondents. Martin must have been happy with this letter, which opens passionately, uses their private slang, 'Buddh', and is playfully mocking – one of her poems is dismissed as 'pukey rubbish'. Somerville cements their bond by 'whispering in your ear' what 'a bore' she finds Miss Newstead, the paid companion her mother obliged her to live with. She ends by inviting Martin into her 'groove', signing off as 'Steadfast', and revealing that she has 'eloped' with Martin's boots. Indeed, Somerville's thoughts are now so fixed on Martin that she cannot end the letter, but draws it out in a postscript, and in the last line is still chasing 'something I wanted to tell you'. (And one has to wonder about her 'little tiny thing'...)

Interior of Colarossis Studio, Paris, pencil on paper, Edith Somerville., Crawford Art Gallery, Cork.

HELL STREET, PARIS
Friday, March 11th '87

My dear girl
Your letter of this morning was as whisky to a thirsty soul where only water is. (This is only a metaphor, and its spiritual tendencies may be attributed to the fact that Newstead and I shared a bottle of beer – at six pence – this evening.) Really you are a good woman to write to me, and likewise to send me the papers which I am awfully glad to get – and was much pleased to see Robert's scratch in the Bat. As for the Oobilee Jode – never was I seen Jode as like. More pukey rubbish could hardly be conceived even by the Dublin beanie [a female servant/small woman].

My dear, I hope yours will be clean out of it – I would be ashamed to see you in such company – How I wish you had dollared the collars. I envy you the leprous paper. This imposing home made thoroughbred silk-all-the-way-up stuff is a rank swindle. The ink darts through it as if it were acid … Your letter interested me so much that before going to my own trivial life I will skim through it again – I have scum.

[…] But now I have to leave the studio earlier in order to practise – after dinner I am working for the Graphic – I have done four of the Irish set – and think they are fairly successful – I ought to be at them now – but you inveigle me into writing to you – bad scran to you. Now let me whisper in your ear, that Newstead is a bore – an amiable, worthy, well meaning, uptight, unexacting creature, but a bore. She is, in a way interesting – I should like to try and write an exhaustive analysis of her character. She has an amazing capacity for doing nothing – literally nothing as I know she doesn't think but sits in a kind of dwam [coma]. […] I must to bed. I cant help it – I don't seem able to write any sort of a decent letter – but I live in a groove and you must get there too, before I can write of anything that will amuse you – Best love from Steadfast – (and my little tiny thing).

Yours Ever
E.OE.S.

P.S. Have you ever discovered that I eloped with your Mc Dermott boots and your bottle of Lively Sarah that you brought that day at the Stores? I am awfully sorry and if there was the parcel post I would send the boots — but as they are too small for me I can't wear them — and now that you are a high toned blue blooded wog [a silly/ jealous girl] I suppose you wouldn't wear them till you came to these wilds. There was something else I wanted to tell you but I can't remember it now.

E.OE.S

Within a few months of this letter, the two were collaborating as Somerville and Ross on their first novel, *An Irish Cousin*. They would collaborate on fourteen more, including their masterpieces, *The Real Charlotte* (1894) and *Some Experiences of an Irish R.M.* (1899). Of their relationship, Somerville wrote: 'For most boys and girls the varying, yet invariable, flirtatious and emotional episodes of youth are resolved and composed by marriage. To Martin and me was opened another way, and the flowering of both our lives was when we met each other.'
[The Selected Letters of Somerville and Ross, edited by Gifford Lewis (Faber & Faber, 1989.]

Grave Stone of Somerville, 1998, John Minihan, black and white photograph., Crawford Art Gallery, Cork.

Oscar Wilde and Constance Holland

Oscar Wilde, just turned 30, is writing to Constance Holland, his wife of six months. Ever the aesthete, he evokes twinned souls, music, the gods and exquisite ecstasy, but the emotion seems generalised. Except for two brief notes, this is the only letter from Wilde to his wife to survive; the rest were probably destroyed by her family after her death.

Tuesday [Postmark 16 December 1884]
THE BALMORAL, EDINBURGH

Dear and Beloved, Here I am, and you at the Antipodes. O execrable facts, that keep our lips from kissing, though our souls are one.

What can I tell you by letter? Alas! Nothing that I would tell you. The messages of the gods to each other travel not by pen and indeed your bodily presence here would not make you more real: for I feel your fingers in my hair, and your cheek brushing mine. The air is full of the music of your voice, my soul and body no longer mine, but mingled in some exquisite ecstasy with yours. I feel incomplete without you. Ever and ever yours

OSCAR
Here I stay till Sunday

16, TITE STREET,
CHELSEA.S.W.

Dear Mr. Humphreys,
It will give me much pleasure to come on Wednesday next. My husband, I am sorry to say, will be out of town.
Yours sincerely
Constance Wilde

Mrs Oscar Wilde

Constance to Arthur Humphreys, the publisher of her compilation of Wildean wit, Oscariana.

Oscar Wilde and Lord Alfred Douglas ('Bosie')

There are no gods, music, or heavenly souls in this letter to Lord Alfred Douglas ('Bosie'), youngest son of the Marquess of Queensbury, but Wilde is clearly distraught with love and passion.
The dashes – highly uncharacteristic of Wilde – convey the rush and tumult in his mind. Wilde is now almost 40 and Douglas, whom he has known almost two years, is 22.

March 1893
SAVOY HOTEL

Dearest of all Boys – Your letter was delightful – red and yellow wine to me – but I am sad and out of sorts – Bosie – you must not make scenes with me – they kill me – they wreck the loveliness of life – I cannot see you, so Greek and gracious, distorted with passion; I cannot listen to your curved lips saying hideous things to me – don't do it – you break my heart – I'd sooner be rented all day, than have you bitter, unjust, and horrid – horrid –

I must see you soon – you are the divine thing I want. – the thing of grace and genius – but I don't know how to do it – Shall I come to Salisbury –? There are many difficulties – my bill here is £49 for a week! I have also got a new sitting-room over the Thames – but you, why are you not here, my dear, my wonderful boy –? I fear I must leave; no money, no credit, and a heart of lead –
Ever your own,

OSCAR

Oscar's obsession with Douglas famously landed him in court in 1895. The night before execution or sentencing frequently focuses the mind on loved ones; here is Wilde, writing to Douglas from Holloway Prison on the eve of his sentencing, seeking to dignify and ennoble their love. He knows that people will judge them and fears he will be condemned as a bad influence; in fact history has pardoned Wilde and judged Douglas as spoilt, vain, parasitic and unworthy (citing as evidence Wilde's extraordinary letter of obsession and recrimination, 'De Profundis'). Yet if Douglas were female, history would certainly have dignified him with the admiring term 'femme fatale'.

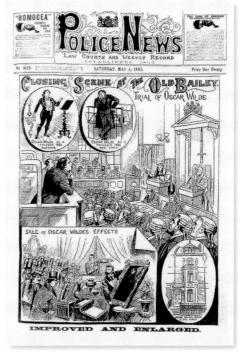

Old Bailey

Monday evening [29 April 1895]
HM PRISON, HOLLOWAY

My dearest boy,
This is to assure you of my immortal, my eternal love for you. Tomorrow all will be over. If prison and dishonour be my destiny, think that my love for you and this idea, this still more divine belief, that you love me in return will sustain me in my unhappiness and will make me capable, I hope, of bearing my grief most patiently. Since the hope, nay rather the certainty, of meeting you again in some world is the goal and the encouragement of my present life, ah! I must continue to live in this world because of that.

Dear –[name deleted by Douglas] came to see me today. I gave him several messages for you. He told me one thing that reassured me; that my mother should never want for anything. I have always provided for her subsistence, and the thought that she might have to suffer privations was making me unhappy. As for you (graceful boy with a Christ-like heart), as for you, I beg you, as soon as you have done all that you can, leave for Italy and regain your calm, and write those lovely poems which you do with such a strange grace. Do not expose yourself to England for any reason whatsoever. If one day, at Corfu or in some enchanted isle, there were a little house where we could live together, oh! life would be sweeter than it has ever been. Your love has broad wings and is strong, your love comes to me through my prison bars and comforts me, your love is the light of all my hours. Those who know not what love is will write, I know, if fate is against us, that I have had a bad influence upon your life. If they do that, you shall write, you shall say in your turn, that it is not so. Our love was always beautiful and noble, and if I have been the butt of a terrible tragedy, it is because the nature of that love has not been understood. In your letter this morning you say something that gives me courage. I must remember it. You write that it is my duty to you and to myself to live in spite of everything. I think that is true. I shall try and I shall do it. I want you to keep Mr Humphreys informed of your movements so that when he comes he can tell me what you are doing. I believe solicitors are allowed to see the prisoners fairly often. Thus I could communicate with you.

I am so happy that you have gone away! I know what that must have cost you. It would have been agony for me to think that you were in England when your name was mentioned in court. I hope you have copies of all my books. All mine have been sold. I stretch out my hands towards you. Oh! May I live to touch your hair and your hands. I think that my love will watch over your life. If I should die, I want you to live a gentle, peaceful existence somewhere, with flowers, books, and lots of work. Try to let me hear from you soon. I am writing you this letter in the midst of great suffering; this long day in court has exhausted me. Dearest boy, sweetest of all young men, most loved and most loveable. Oh! wait for me! wait for me! I am now, as ever since the day we met, yours devotedly and with an immortal love

OSCAR

In fact the jury couldn't agree on a verdict, and Wilde's trial was adjourned. On the 3rd of May he was released on bail. Douglas was in France; he had wanted to give evidence but was advised against by Wilde's lawyers and persuaded to leave the country. Here, in one of his few letters to survive, he writes begging Wilde to skip bail and join him.

Oscar Wilde; Lord Alfred Bruce Douglas by Gillman & Co, silver gelatin print, May 1893, © National Portrait Gallery. London.

[May 1895]

It seems dreadful to be here without you but I hope you will join me next week. Do keep up your spirits, my dearest darling.

I continue to think of you day and night, and send you all my love.

I am always your own loving and devoted boy,

Bosie

Wilde wrote back that it was 'nobler and more beautiful to stay [...] A false name, a disguise, a hunted life, all that is not for me'. He also thought he might be acquitted, but he got two years of hard labour. On leaving prison, he was given the opportunity by his forgiving wife to return to her, providing he renounce Douglas. He could not and the pair lived together, on and off and acrimoniously, until Wilde's death in 1900.

[The Complete Letters of Oscar Wilde, edited by Merlin Holland and Rupert Hart-Davies, Fourth Estate, 2000.]

George Egerton
and Reginald Golding Bright

In this letter the 42-year-old writer, George Egerton (Mary Chavelita Dunne), is all at once mothering, cajoling and seducing the 27-year-old London theatrical agent, Reginald Golding Bright. More than age separates them: Egerton was a feminist who had many lovers (including Nobel Laureate Knut Hamsun) and was about to divorce her second husband; Golding was sexually inexperienced and suffering some kind of nervous breakdown. He sent Egerton flowers and pledged his platonic devotion, but apparently shirked carnal love. In this letter Egerton knows that he is seeking 'motherliness' and addresses him as her 'good little son', but she is also clear that 'love is something apart from platonics' and taunts him with her Norwegian lover, Ole, who wants her 'as a wife' (i.e. sexually). This curious letter is half-maternal, half-amorous; in one line she's suggesting gently that Golding is mistaken in his feelings, in the next she's artfully encouraging him on.

21 February 1901

Good little son, curious tangle of affection, I have read your long letter through twice. I am grateful to you, boy, for much kind dear thought of me in it, but in some ways you mistake. A mistake arising out of my too great reticence as to my own feelings. I have felt and feel a difficulty and if you had not overcome your dumbness enough to attack me as it were on this point, should not speak of it now. I know you do so because you care for me in a strange beautiful way, a way I care greatly to have.

    […]You write of love that is the love of a healthy-souled man and woman in a way to make me believe you have no idea of what love is. To Ole [her Norwegian lover], loving me as he does no relationship other than wife would be possible, and rightly so. Love is something apart from platonics … Your attitude is born of solitude, of an almost morbid desire to protect and love without letting anything other than the spiritual side of affection dominate. Boy dear, you will know better some day when the right woman comes.

[…] I have gipsy traits in me, an artist to the finger-tips, vagabond blood not a little – but I am a woman and I need love as few women. I have found no man love me long platonically. You are safeguarded by your care for another – and your need for my motherliness, yet you miss me after the few times I have been with you. You let me play a part in your thought disproportionate to your feeling for me. You try to anticipate my wishes, you trouble more about me than I trouble over myself, you torture yourself with doubts, fears concerning me. You cry at the very thought of my death. My dear, good little son, I have no fear. I am impersonal even in thinking of myself. I have let you do more for me than I have ever let anyone do, because I believe it is good for you to come out of that place of despondency in which you were sitting in the dark. I could make you laugh and rejoice and think life good if I were to see you oftener. That I came in when I did is written for some purpose. I would not be patient with your weakness long, I have sharp angles, hardnesses too, and you have too good, too big a heart to fossilize as you are doing. I shall expect much from you – not for myself or in relationship to myself – but for yourself. Your care for others might only produce weakness in them. I no longer believe in abnegation nor renunciation. All my sacrifices have been useless – harmful often, destructive of forces I might have held in reserve to help others wisely – one pamperizes and demoralizes others. I now try to help others to help themselves. […] Do not fret or trouble about me. I dree my weird [sic]. You have been a dear son to me and I am grateful for what I have taken from you because I feel you loved to give to me. If you want anything from me, ask, or I shall feel hurt. What I said to you I meant as long as I am here below, come to me as often as you will. Realize I have no fear of anything. I have missed you today. There is a confession.

[…] I have hardly thanked you for all your pretty thought of me, your flowers and books and tender care but believe me I am none the less grateful. […] Dear glad, hopeful good boy, life has much in it. Don't fret over the little mother, she has always gone her own gait. Don't fancy she is going to leave you awhile. There is more for her to do. She bids you good-morning, comes to your side and stoops down and rubs out all the wrinkles and hopes you are not tired and tells you to be strong and sensible and glad, above all glad. Her kind boy! Shut your eyes and I will smooth my hands over your hair, your little Mother.

The 'little mother' and 'her kind boy' were married five months later. He was her third husband and her last; the marriage was not successful but continued until their deaths within four years of each other in the 1940s.

[A Leaf from the Yellow Book, the Correspondence of George Egerton *(edited Terence de Vere White (The Richards Press, 1958).]*

Mary Chevilita Dunne (George Egerton)
by Walter Benington,
© National Portrait Gallery, London.

Annie O'Donnell and James Phelan

Twenty-one-year-old nursery maid and Galway native, Annie O'Donnell, is writing from Pittsburgh to 25-year-old James Phelan, a Kilkenny farmer settled in Indianapolis, whom she met three years earlier on the crossing from Ireland. He initiated the correspondence out of the blue and she responded, though she admitted frankly that after the three-year gap she 'barely remembered your face ...

and have but the slightest idea of what you looked like'. Because they hardly know each other, she provides here a brief life history, gives her vital statistics and reveals poignant emigrant longing for home. Annie was reserved and sensible; none of her letters is very demonstrative, but she is careful to get across her virtues – loyalty, reserve and steadfastness. The aim is not to seduce as a lover, but to present her wifely credentials.

PITTSBURGH PA
Oct. 18th 1901

My dear Jim,

It is almost time that I should answer your letter, I know you will think me very neglectful for not answering much sooner which I intended doing, but I assure you I have been quite busy and the little spare time I get which is usually at night I give to sewing. Since our folks went to Buffalo and left us with the children, you know we feel a big responsibility.

You seem to think your letters in the past were not very acceptable, but that is not so, for I would never have answered them if I had thought that. It is very hard to please in letters I do know, but must say yours are too interesting to leave unanswered even if it takes me a long time to do so. It is not through lack of thought, for if I did not care for a person, I would never condescend to put my thoughts on paper.

Life seems just the same old way here. I have been out just twice since, had a pretty good time. Everybody seemed glad to see me back. Spent one Sunday with my sisters who wanted to know all about the Indiana letter they got for me. We talked a good deal of you. They live opposite the Union Station where we parted that day pretty near three years ago. There is a new depot built there now, yes, one of the finest I have seen in my travels.

I have two sisters here, both married long before I dreamt of leaving home. One, the eldest of our whole family, has two little girls and a boy and the other has a boy and girl. I was but a mere child when they left for America. Neither of us knew the other when we met. I am the baby girl of the family. There is only one boy younger and he is the real baby although he is about sixteen. We had in our home originally five girls and two boys, but they are almost all far apart now. All my sisters being married but one. Father and mother still living. I hear from them quite often.

I was born in a little place called Spiddal about twenty miles from Galway City. My parents always wished me to be a school teacher, so at the age of thirteen, they sent me to the Convent of the Presentation (Galway) where I was appointed monitor which position I held till October of '98. I did not board at the Convent but simply went there to school, and it is there that those dear happy days I told you of were spent.

When I left there, I made my debut in this world and not until I reached Pittsburgh did I know of that selfish deceit etc. that rules this world. It was then that I missed everything, for I was thrown entirely on my own resources. And it was there also I chose my friends (very few), became independent and reserved and have been so ever since. When I met Ellen, I met the one I often wished for. She is dignified and won't associate with everyone, and she is one of the three in my whole life that won my entire affection, a thing which is rather difficult to do, but once done is done forever.

In the winter of '98 I weighed 116 pounds. A year later 127, later still 137½ then came down to 120, but I have grown quite tall since you saw me, my height being somewhere round 5'6' or perhaps a little more.

Well now, Jim, I think I have told you most every little thing of interest, so you will please excuse me for my mistakes as am in quite a hurry as usual, and hope you will write me very soon. I suppose I don't need to tell you to remember me to anybody. I get my share of teasing here about the little print letters from Indianapolis, but I never mind. I am always glad to get them and do write a long one very soon.

Will now close with love x
from Annie

After three years of this epistolary courtship (during which they barely met), Annie and Jim were married in 1904, settled in Pittsburgh and had eight children, six surviving to adulthood. Annie died in 1959, aged 80, and Jim died two years later.

[Your Fondest Annie, letters from Annie O'Donnell to James P. Phelan 1901–1904, *edited Maureen Murphy, University College Dublin Press, 2005.*]

An early view of Pittsburgh railway.

Hanna Sheehy and Frank Skeffington

The incipient 24-year-old suffragette, Hanna Sheehy, is writing a late-night, sometimes indecipherable and ungrammatical letter to her slightly younger fiancé, Frank Skeffington. They have recently graduated from UCD where Skeffington's intellect so impressed that his friend James Joyce named him the second smartest man in college. Hanna was the eldest of the four Sheehy girls, whose lively house served as a social centre for undergraduates – Joyce sang at their soirées and later mined the whole family for his fiction.

Intellectually Hanna and Frank were well-suited, and she took on his feminism, socialism and, eventually, atheism, but they argued frequently and passionately. She writes here after one such argument. The alternation between self-reproach and recrimination, and the hopeful striving towards mutual improvement is characteristic of their correspondence.

Sunday Oct. 27 [1901]
11.30 p.m.

My own darling Frank,

I hope you have not been unwell today, love, & that you got rid of your cold by the rest in bed. You did look unwell last night. I don't know how it was, love, but I turned away from you last night very angry & choking with a horrible mixture of pain & rage too! Then today I was very hurt & bitter – until about one, darling & then the revulsion sets in & I have been happy, yet self-reproachful, all day & longing to see you, sweetheart. My own Frank, I know more then ever I cannot live without you, [as] you without me either – that's my joy. And, though my faults grieve you so much dear, try to help me to correct them & bear with them as you always have done. And, as for yours, dear, I'll try to be steadier & stronger, for I know I can help you fight your weaknesses & up to this I have merely wavered from one extreme to the other. I waited until I had things fully thought out before writing, so I can't post now but you'll get it as soon as I can give it all the same & it soothes me to write it before I go to bed.

Now, love, first about my health. Forgive my words of yesterday. The 'hammering' does get on me nerves, sometimes, Frank. I must say, & I really think you worry too much over me. It doesn't do me any good either, for, you know, over-anxiety generally seems exaggeration & so fails. Will you leave good old nature & my 'line of country ancestors' to work their slow, but sure way? I'll do [illegible] & keep those rules, – food, walking & sleeping & at the end of every month if you don't find me better I'll submit to a scolding. But now, this time I was better; my backache never comes lately & generally I feel brighter so won't you be patient with me!

Then, Frank, as to [whether?] I work if I agree to leave it all in your hands, dear, will it lose your time? Would it be better to write just? But that you will have already considered.

Now, on my side, if you take it up you must be more regular, dear, & above all get me to be so – about rising & all that. Then about the work, you are grand sometimes – usually in the beginning, love, pardon my saying all this – but then we both flag a little & get out of form. You or I get tired & that is depressing on the other. And so on. Sometimes I read a novel, sometimes

James Joyce

117

you have played chess & feel lazy just. You know, dear. Well, we must both struggle against all that. I must discuss things with you as much as I can & learn to put my side with more logic & without [regret?] if you oppose me. For I must help you at your own – our – plans for the writing & the future generally, husband, dear. So, darling, if you agree to take up the charge & be strong, well, I'll give it to you freely & you can do as you please about my health, love, if you see me over-straining it.

That is the true course & you were right. We ought not to admit failure, but work together & then if we fail we'll fail together, dear.

I have looked into my heart well today, dear & I see that without your help & love my life & work are useless, though of course, you will see too that I should find it hard not to work my best this year as well as after our marriage, Frank. I hope that may not be my fate ever, darling – to be cut off from work – but even if so, I pray that I may be able to bear it cheerfully with the help of Love.

Your words of reproach ring in my ears ever since – 'Hanna, Hanna, Hanna!' My Frank forgive the pain I caused you, Goodnight,

Your own devoted Hanna

Photograph of the Sheehy sisters, Hanna, Mary and Kathleen, and an unidentified woman
Reproduced from the original held in the Curran Collection at UCD Library Special Collections
by kind permission of Helen Solterer.

Frank, writing nine months later, addresses Hanna as 'wife' although they have just come through a painful episode which threatened (though not seriously) their engagement. He begins by brilliantly evoking an unexpected meeting on the street – he was thinking of her and she appeared – before moving on to the familiar territory of his 'fatal domineering disposition'. His concern about this was touching, probably excessive, and certainly unusual in an Edwardian man; Hanna, who went to prison in 1912 for suffragette activities, credited Frank with her commitment to the cause. During their three-year courtship they analysed each other's characters and their relationship exhaustively – this letter is rushed because Frank was trying to catch the post; after sending it off, he immediately started another long letter, marked 6.30 p.m.

RANELAGH
6/6/[1902]
4.20 p.m.

My beloved wife,

The post leaves early in this quarter so I have only till five to write to you. I haven't very much to say, though, sweetheart; I am full of joy at the swift and complete removal of a terrible cloud, but too full of it to speak or write much. Shall I tell you what I was thinking of as I walked down Rutland Square that first time, never dreaming that you were at my heels? I felt sure you would have come back to me sometime, but I couldn't tell when; I was fancying the separation over, the return of rings & all the rest of it. Then I fancied myself telling you that I'd always wait, and promising to let you know my address wherever I might go. Then I was changing my address from one part of London to another, and sending you word every time; then I was beginning to go further afield, when – you touched me & woke me up. So I hadn't to notify you of many changes of address, dear!

Oh, my love, my love, what would I do without you? What a blank my whole life would be! How completely all my designs and aspirations would fall to pieces, if the all-supporting central pivot were removed! But Hanna darling I mustn't think of that only, though it is what presents itself to me most forcibly after my escape from the danger. The worst of what you said to me, love, is that much of it is true. I have too often forgotten, my darling, the promise I made on the day of

Hanna Sheehy (on right) and friends.

Hanna Sheehy and son.

our betrothal, that there should be no master in our union. I will try to remember it better in future. I will try all the harder because I feel that in any case, no matter what I may do to you, you are mine for ever, – just as I am yours, under all circumstances, my own angel. I will try very hard, my sweet Hanna, to conquer that fatal domineering disposition that has so often brought tears to your eyes. I will try very hard, my own Hanna, to keep that evil temper from fighting against your ideas and your individuality, – which in my heart I always respect, Hanna, even when my reckless words are buffeting you. I will try very hard, Hanna, not because you wanted to leave me, but because you came back. I will try very hard! Help me!

I have a dread about this letter being opened; I hope you will be on the look-out for it, – and maybe for one in the morning, sweetest, though I'm not sure if I can get it posted. Anyhow I'll certainly meet you, my darling, in the morning.

So good-bye for a short time, my heart's queen, my own true, fond wife, mine for ever and ever!

Your passionately loving
Frank
Kisses, dearest, on your beloved name.

On their marriage in 1903, they combined their names to Sheehy-Skeffington to symbolize the equality of their relationship. Together they co-founded the Irish Women's Franchise League; co-edited the suffragist weekly, *The Irish Citizen*; supported the strikers in the 1913 Lock Out; opposed the Great War; and went (separately) on hunger strike. True to his pacifist views, Frank took no part in the Easter Rising but was arrested while attempting to prevent looting and executed by an officer subsequently judged insane. Hanna refused all offers of compensation from the governemnt. She raised their only child, Owen (who became a senator), and continued their political work, growing rather more, not less, radical and intransigent with age. She missed Frank's humorous, tempering influence – in one letter he accuses her of lacking all sense of humour – and his murder understandably embittered her.

[Sheehy-Skeffington Correspondence, *NLI, MS 40, 461 / 2 and MS 40,464 / 11.*]

W.B. Yeats and Maud Gonne

In this letter, William Butler Yeats is begging his muse, Maud Gonne, not to marry the nationalist and Boer War hero, John MacBride. All three are in their late thirties, and Yeats has been proposing marriage and writing poems and plays to Gonne for fourteen years. He has tolerated her French lover and child, but now threatens to break off all contact if she marries MacBride – and then crosses out the threat. This tortured letter makes appeal to Gonne's social and political ideals, not her heart. After invoking spirits and visions, Yeats argues that marriage between the upper-class Protestant Gonne and the Catholic petit-bourgeois MacBride would be a *mésalliance* which 'the people' would never accept. He's transposing his own feelings onto 'the people'. Is he conscious of this? The angry repetition of the word 'thrust' is revealing. Is it really MacBride's social status he objects to, or is he just jealous? Is he being evasive by focusing on the 'people', rather than his own feelings? Or is this a noble attempt to think beyond himself to what's best for Gonne, and for their mutual concern – Ireland? Does he have a gut instinct against the marriage, which he is failing to express well? Probably all of these. And at the deepest level, he's incubating poetry: the last line looks forward 35 years to 'The Circus Animals' Desertion': 'I thought my dear must her own soul destroy'.

Few of Yeats' letters to Gonne have survived; this one did because he chanced to write a draft into a notebook.

[LONDON?]
[Late January 1903?]

< I appeal to you in the name of 14 years of friendship to read this letter. It is perhaps the last thing I shall [write] to you.> [Crossed out]

Dear Friend,

      I thought over things last night. The thought came to me 'you are not writing to her quite fully what you think. You fear to make her angry, to spoil her memory of you. Write all [deletions] that you would have her know. Not to do so is mere selfishness. It is too late now to think of anything but the truth. If you do not speak no one will.' Then I thought that you had given me the right to speak. I remembered the passage in one of the diaries in which I have written all that was of the moment in our dealing with spiritual things. (I have left out some expressions of feeling that might give you pain.) Here is the passage it is dated December 12 1898. 'I will write what has happened that I may read of it in coming years & re[mem]ber all the rest. [deletions] On the morning of Dec. 7 I woke after a sleep less broken than my sleep is commonly & knew that our lips had met in dreams. I went to see her & she said "What dreams had you last night?" I told her what had happened & she said "I was with you last night but do not remember much," but in the evening she said some such words as these. "I will tell you what happened last night I went out of my body. I saw my body from outside it & I was brought away by Lug [Celtic God] & my hand [deletions] was put in yours & I was told that we were married. All became dark. I think we went away together to do some work."' There are other entries [similar] concerning this & earlier visions of mine. Now I claim that this gives me the right to speak. Your hands were put in mine & we were told to do a certain great work together. For all who undertake such tasks there comes a moment of extreme peril. I know now that you have come to your moment of peril. If you carry out your purpose you will fall into a lower order & do great injury to the religion of free souls that is growing up in Ireland, it may be to enlighten the whole world. A man said to me last night having seen the announcement [of the Gonne-MacBride engagement] in the papers 'The priests will exult over us all for generations because of this.' There are people (& these are the great number) who need the priests or some other masters but [there] are a few bid me write this letter. You possess your influence in Ireland very largely because you come to the people from above. You represent a superior class, a class whose people are more independent, have a more beautiful life, a more refined life. Every man almost of the people who has spoken to me of you has shown that you influence him very largely because of this. [deletion] Maud Gonne is surrounded with romance. She puts from her what seems an easy & splendid life that she may devote herself to the people. I have heard you called 'our great lady'. But Maud Gonne is about to pass away […] you are going to marry one of the people [deletion]. This weakness which has [thrust?] down your soul to a lower order of faith is thrusting you down socially is thrusting you down to the people. [Deletions] They will never forgive it – This most aristocratic minded [,] the more thirsting for what is above them & beyond them, of living peoples. […] You and I were chosen to begin this work & just when I come to understand it fully you go from me & seek to thrust the people further down into weakness further from self-reliance. Now on a matter on which I must speak if I am to say & believe that some are more than man now I appeal, I whose hands were placed in yours by eternal hands, to come back to yourself. To take up again the proud solitary haughty life that made [you] seem like one of the Golden Gods. Do not, you [who] seem the most strong, the most inspired be the first to betray us, to betray the truth. Become again as one of the Gods. Is it the priest, when the day of great hazard has come who will lead the people. No no. He will palter with the government [as] he did at the act of union [deletion]. He will say 'Be quiet, be good Christians, do not shed blood.' [Is it] not the priest who has [softened] the will of our young men – who has broken their pride. You have said all these things & not so long ago. For [it] is not only the truth & your friends but your own soul that you are about to betray.

Iseult Gonne, by Paula McGloin

W.B.Yeats

She replied quickly, as she always did to him, to say that her mind was made up, but that her action would have no consequences for their friendship or her status. About to go through with a life-altering event, she yet expects her life to remain unaltered (except for a change of religion). It is a curious letter from a woman two weeks before her wedding. The subtext is clear – she is not in love with MacBride (whom she never mentions) and won't be moulding her life to his. Yeats kept all Gonne's letters; most, like this one, are warm, confiding, reliant on his support, and adroit at feeding his conception of her. Here she plays on his ideal of her as 'the soul of the crowd' to get round his contempt for Catholicism.

Maud Gonne

5 RUE DU PARADIS
LAVAL MAYEUNE
10th Feby [1903]

My dear Friend,

     I have your three letters – they have made me sad, because I fear that you are sad & yet our friendship need not suffer by my marriage. You have known me for many years in the ups & downs of a rather agitated life, yet you have always found me the same as far as our friendship was concerned. So it will always be. I did not myself quite understand things but I know that I am fulfilling a destiny & but for the sorrow I have in giving pain, I am at peace with myself.

     About my changing religion I believe like you that there is one great universal truth. God that pervades everything, I believe that each religion is a different prism through which one looks at truth. None can see the whole of truth. When we do, we shall have merged in the deity, & we shall be as God but that is not yet. In the meantime our nation looks at God or truth through one prism, The Catholic Religion –

I am officially a protestant & supposed to look at it from another & much narrower one which is narrower than the English one. I prefer to look at truth through the same prism as my country people – I am going to become a Catholic. It seems to me of small importance if one calls the great spirit forces the Sidhe, the Gods & the Arch Angels, the great symbols of all religions are the same –

But I do feel it important not to belong to the Church of England. You say I leave the few to mix myself in the crowd while Willie I have always told you I am the voice, the soul of the crowd.

I will be here at Laval for the next 10 or 12 days, it is a lovely peaceful place here where I can play with Iseult & forget for a little the worries of life.

Friend of mine *au revoir*. I shall go over to Ireland in a couple of months, if you care to see me I shall be so glad & you will find I think that I am just the same woman you have always known, marriage won't change me I think at all. I intend to keep my own name & to go on with all my work the same as ever.

Write to me sometimes for I want your news & want to keep your friendship always.

Maud Gonne

Yeats was right to warn against the marriage, which went sour almost immediately. However, he was wrong about Gonne's reputation suffering, and conversely she was proved right about 'fulfilling a destiny': MacBride redeemed years of drunkenness and lechery by fighting an excellent Rising and bravely facing death by firing squad, thus bequeathing Maud Gonne MacBride iconic status as a 1916 widow. She and Yeats continued to correspond until his death. The constant reiteration of 'friendship' in their letters is revealing; Yeats is unusual among artists in that his muse was also his best friend. For fifty years they shared their concerns, great and small, and were tolerant and understanding of each other. In their own Golden Dawn way, their partnership was as equal as the Sheehy-Skeffingtons.

W.B. Yeats and Margot Ruddock

Yeats' last proposal to Maud Gonne was in 1916; as usual she refused so he proposed to her daughter, Iseult, who also refused. Instead he married 24-year-old George Hyde-Lees, who ensured his continued attention by having visions. The marriage was happy, but Yeats still needed muses. Here he is, at 69, internationally famous as a Nobel Laureate, writing in excitement to the 27-year-old married English actress, Margot Ruddock, who looked not unlike the young Maud Gonne. In this enthusiastic letter, he dedicates verse to her, hints at intrigue, promises to be more energetic next time they meet and boasts of feeling love before first sight. Were they having a full-on affair? Probably not. But he was enjoying the effects of his recent Steinach ('monkey gland') operation for sexual potency, and was carrying on similar amatory correspondences with two other young women at this time.

November 13 [1934]
KILDARE STREET CLUB, DUBLIN C.17

My dearest,

Tell me about Sunday night, about the Eliot dance play? I expected from an horoscope a postponement to Easter. It is as well for it will leave December to us. I wonder if you would think out the singing or speaking of (say) half a dozen of my poems. I shall probably bring over a zither that we can use at the Abbey with Dulac's music. I will be able perhaps to introduce you as a 'sayer' of my verse before the play begins. The B.B.C might help. Half a dozen poems in a studied order, with variety and climax.

I have in my head two poems 'for Margot' but I may not write them yet. A long toil on the play has tired me and I want the rest of practical work or of a change to prose. I must not meet you again a tired man. However the play opens with a song partly addressed to you.

I
Every loutish lad in love
Thinks his wisdom great enough
(What cares love for this and that?)
All the town to set astare
As though Pythagoras wandered there
(Crown of gold or dung of swine)

II
Should old Pythagoras fall in love
Little may he boast thereof
(What cares love for this and that?)
Days go by in foolishness
But O how great the sweetness is
(Crown of gold or dung of swine)/

III
Open wide those gleaming eyes
That can make the loutish wise
(What cares love for this and that?)
Make a leader of the schools
Thank the Lord all men are fools
(Crown of gold or dung of swine)

Crown of gold, etc. prepares for something in the play.
I shall not comment on the word 'intrigue', but I have looked it up in a French dictionary (I forgot to do it this morning). The English word is certainly not an alternative to 'no word at all'.

I must wind up my letter. Lennox Robinson and Peak and Bowl or Boule – I think that is how they write their names, which sound like something very improper out of 'The Golden Bough' – our new producer and designer, arrive in a few minutes to decide on our next production. They obliterated the offence of their *Macbeth* by a magnificent performance of *The School for Wives* last night, excellent in acting, magnificent in costume and scenery, costume and scenery were black and white throughout. I am greatly comforted, for I rammed them down the throat of my committee and after *Macbeth* I thought my instinct had failed me. In all that has to do with human beings I am a gambler. I chose Lennox Robinson as manager before we had exchanged sentences by the shape of his back. How did you and I choose each other? I think even before we had seen each other's faces. Yours always,

W.B.Y

Write an occasional letter to me at Riversdale, Rathfarnham, Dublin. My wife knows that we work on the theatre project. It is more natural if you write there.

Margot, like most of Yeats' flirtations, wanted to be a writer and her letters to him generally concern her work and are not intimate. But in February 1936, probably sensing his declining interest in her, she went all out to reignite his passion.

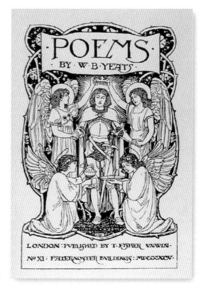

Poems *by W. B. Yeats*

14 WESTBOURNE GARDENS
Saturday Evening [1 February 1936]

Darling Yeats,

On Friday morning at ten minutes to ten as I was on my way to my dairy to shop I had the most extraordinary experience. You definitely appeared in a sort of mental vision, and you got up from a bed. I stood quite still, it was so tremendous a thing. I shook all over, you looked and kept on looking at me. You went on for about five whole minutes, which is a very long time when thinking, and I made my way into the milk shop in a state of complete dream and didn't know what to buy!

I came back and told Raymond [her husband] I was worried and then thought shall I wire him, then I thought no I won't, it may not mean anything – so I went out to tea with some people. When I returned Raymond came in with a newspaper and said, 'You were right about Yeats, he is seriously ill again.' I had to ring up, which I did, and the next morning I wired I was coming because I simply had to. Hope I didn't seem indiscreet. I wouldn't have done so for the world but for what had happened. I do hope you are better and will get better.

If you want me, and circumstances are such, I may come. Any time you wire I will come. If you don't, I am thinking of you just the same.

Margot

She was not the first woman to try to get Yeats' attention by having visions but it didn't work. He replied to this breathless letter coolly, keeping her firmly at a distance – 'My wife has arrived on Sunday and has taken charge' – and followed up with a letter about her work, generous in its length and frankness, but damning in its conclusions: 'I do not like your recent poems [...] you take the easiest course [...] because – damn you – you are lazy.' A month later she had a nervous breakdown. Yeats paid for her treatment, but told his friend Olivia Shakespear, 'I want to keep at a distance from a tragedy where I can be no further help'. Margot recovered briefly, but relapsed, and a year later was committed permanently to an asylum where she died in 1951, twelve years after Yeats.

[Ah Sweet Dancer, W.B. Yeats and Margot Ruddock, a Correspondence, *edited by Roger McHugh, Macmillan, 1970.*]

James Joyce and Nora Barnacle

The 22-year-old James Joyce is writing with uncharacteristic diffidence to the Galway chamber maid, Nora Barnacle, who has failed to show up for their first date. He blames himself – 'I may be blind' – and throws himself on her mercy, begging her to make another appointment. She did. They met the next day, on the 16th of June 1904, now the most famous date in Irish literary history.

15 June 1904

60 SHELBOURNE ROAD

I may be blind. I looked for a long time at a head of reddish-brown hair and decided it was not yours. I went home quite dejected. I would like to make an appointment but it might not suit you. I hope you will be kind enough to make one with me – if you have not forgotten me!

James A. Joyce

Four months later she agreed to follow him into exile (without marriage); they eventually settled in Trieste, had two children, and were never apart until Joyce's visit to Dublin in 1909 to further the publication of *Dubliners*. There he was prey to the malice of a 'friend', Vincent Cosgrave, who insinuated that Nora had been two-timing him during the precious summer of 1904. This extraordinary letter veers between obscenity and deep spiritual love; Joyce is at once aroused by the thought of Nora with another – he demands to know all the details – and devastated by her betrayal which threatens the foundations of his life and work.

7 August 1909
44 FONTENOY STREET

It is half past six in the morning and I am writing in the cold. I have hardly slept all night.

Is Georgie my son? The first night I slept with you in Zurich was October 11th and he was born July 27th. That is nine months and 16 days. I remember that there was very little blood that night. Were you fucked by anyone before you came to me? You told me that a gentleman named Holohan (a good Catholic, of course, who makes his Easter duty regularly) wanted to fuck you when you were in that hotel, using what they call a 'French letter'. Did he do so? Or did you allow him only to fondle you and feel you with his hands?

Tell me. When you were in that field near the Dodder (on the nights when I was not there) with that other (a 'friend' of mine) were you lying down when you kissed? Did you place your hand on him as you did on me in the dark and did you say to him as you did to me 'What is it, dear?' One day I went up and down the streets of Dublin hearing nothing but those words, saying them over and over again to myself and standing still to hear better the voice of my love.

What is to become of my love now? How am I to drive away the face which will come now between our lips? Every second night along the same streets! I have been a fool. I thought that all the time you gave yourself only to me and you were dividing your body between me and another. In Dublin here the rumour here is circulated that I have taken the leavings of others. Perhaps they laugh when they see me parading 'my' son in the streets.

O Nora! Nora! Nora! I am speaking now to the girl I loved, who had red-brown hair and sauntered over to me and took me so easily into her arms and made me a man.

I will leave for Trieste as soon as Stannie sends me the money, and then we can arrange what is best to do.

O, Nora, is there any hope yet of my happiness? Or is my life to be broken? They say here that I am in consumption. If I could forget my books and my children and forget that the girl I loved was false to me and remember her only as I saw her with the eyes of my boyish love I would go out of life content. How old and miserable I feel!

JIM

His misapprehension was fast cleared up. The next day, a friend, John Byrne, told him Cosgrave's brag was a 'blasted lie', and his brother Stanislaus wrote the same from Trieste, as did Nora in a short letter which has not been preserved but which cut Joyce 'to the quick': 'As long as I live I shall always remember the quiet dignity of that letter, its sadness and scorn, and the utter humiliation it caused me. She asks me to forget the ignorant Galway girl that came across my life and says I am not kind to her.'

Nora Barnacle

The joy of their reunion freed him to express transgressive sexual fantasies; she replied in kind and they embarked on perhaps the most obscene correspondence in literary history. The following letter was written in a lull coming down from sexual frenzy; Joyce is now anxious to emphasize the spiritual side of his love. He has made a pilgrimage to her maid's quarters in Finn's hotel where she worked when they first met, and writes of approaching her small bed with the wonder of the Magi approaching the manger. His feeling for the room's pitiful modesty and for her forlorn state is greatly moving – then as now, Clongowes boys did not commit for life to orphaned Galway chambermaids.

11 December 1909
44 FONTENOY STREET, DUBLIN

My dearest Nora

No letter again from you tonight. You have not answered.

 The four Italians have left Finn's Hotel and live now over the show. I paid about £20 to your late mistress, returning good for evil. Before I left the hotel I told the waitress who I was and asked her to let me see the room you slept in. She brought me upstairs and took me to it. You can imagine my excited appearance and manner. I saw my love's room, her bed, the four little walls within which she dreamed of my eyes and voice, the little curtains she pulled aside in the morning to look out at the grey sky of Dublin, the poor modest silly things on the walls over which her glance travelled while she undressed her fair young body at night.

 Ah not lust, dearest, not the wild brutal madness I have written to you these last days and nights, not the wild beast-like desire for your body, dearest, is what drew me to you then and holds me to you now. No, dearest, not that at all but a most tender, adoring, pitiful love for your youth and girlhood and weakness. O the sweet pain you brought into my heart! O the mystery your voice speaks to me of!

 Tonight I will not write to you as I have done before. All men are brutes, dearest, but at least in me there is also something higher at times. Yes, I too have felt at moments the burning in my soul of that pure and sacred fire which burns for ever on the altar of my love's heart. I could have knelt by the little bed and abandoned myself to a flood of tears. The tears were besieging my eyes as I stood looking at it. I could have knelt and prayed there as the three kings from the East knelt and prayed before the manger in which Jesus lay. They had travelled over deserts and seas and brought their gifts and wisdom and royal trains to kneel before a little new-born child and I had brought my errors and follies and sins and wondering and longing to lay them at the little bed in which a young girl had dreamed of me.

Dearest, I am so sorry I have not even a poor five lire note to send you tonight but on Monday I will send you one. I leave for Cork tomorrow morning but I would prefer to be going westward, towards those strange places whose names thrill me on your lips, Oughterard, Clare-Galway, Coleraine, Oranmore, towards those wild fields of Connacht in which God made to grow 'my beautiful wild flower of the hedges, my dark-blue rain-drenched flower'.

JIM

Crisis and excitement over, Joyce returned to his impecunious and peripatetic family life. He and Nora finally married in a London registry office on the 4th of July 1831, ten years before his death in Zurich. She survived another ten years. As the inspiration for Molly Bloom and Anna Livia Plurabelle, she is one of art's most important muses, but was luckier than most; she was never simply an ideal or an expendable source of inspiration. Franz Liszt's epitaph for Harriet Smithson (see p.72) applies to many muses, but not to Nora Barnacle.

Contemporary portrait of Joyce and Barnacle by John Nolan.

George Moore and Lady Maud Cunard

The 54-year old bachelor novelist, George Moore, is writing one of his regular letters to Maud, Lady Cunard, an Irish-American heiress 20 years his junior. After marrying (unhappily) into the shipping Cunards, Maud grew into a noted London society hostess and art patron.

Moore had been her romantic slave since she cried out on their first meeting in 1894: 'George Moore, you have a soul of fire!' Here he opens with a wonderfully graceful acknowledgement that his love exceeds hers, but that it is more fortunate to feel love than to inspire it. Some men, writers in particular, seem to prefer unattainable women, but Moore is unusual in admitting so frankly that it is the 'hardness' of his muse that holds him captive.

9 January 1906
4, UPPER ELY PLACE, DUBLIN

My dear,

I write to you because I am thinking of you. As I sit by the fire I seem to see you like a star in a dark sky – my star, that one which I must follow. No man has absorbed you as you have absorbed me and I am sorry, for it must be lonely to live in the dark, to see no star ahead of one. Other men have wives, children, religion, God. I have my star, an ideal, my ideal of light, loveliness and grace which I follow always and which I shall see shining when my eyes grow dim and spectacle is about to fade out of them for ever. I am writing the Avignon episode, for it served to show me how inveterate my admiration and my love for you are. They are as inherent, as much part of me, as Ingres, Manet, Shelley, Balzac or Tourgueneff – more than they. When I have written this story in your honour I am going to write a pamphlet entitled *Fairwell*; it will I think make a noise in the world. But I care very little whether it does or doesn't …I am thinking now of those days at Holt when your mother's boxes arrived and we unpacked them together. The pretty May sunlight was dancing in the trees, and along the grass 'the lilacs bloomed in the courtyard'. And that reminds me of – not the variorum edition of Whitman but the edition of Poe which you sent me and which I cannot lay my hands on. Your dear mother we shall never see again! How strange it seems, and in the three weeks I spent at Holt I seemed to have learnt to know her so well, better possibly than I know anything else. I suppose that is why I think about her so much. You are a hard woman in many ways, but if you were less hard I don't think you would have held me captive such a long time; I do not complain of my captivity – good heavens no; it is the only allegiance I acknowledge, and man without an allegiance is like a ball of thistledown. My thoughts are always like thistledown – a thought of Harry Lynch has darted across my mind. It is perfectly disgraceful that I have not sent him *The Lake* [Moore's most famous novel]. Of course you know that he knows the lake as well as I do, every island, every shore – I must send him the book tomorrow. I have written page after page without speaking of Mrs Cotton. Is she out of danger? Her recovery shows how little doctors know of life and death, how inscrutable are the two great mysteries. When you see her will you tell her how much I rejoice in her recovery. I should like to write myself and I would if I knew her out of danger.

As ever,
George Moore

Lady Cunard separated from her husband in 1911 but did not marry Moore. Their relationship possibly never went beyond platonic though he liked to encourage the rumour that he was father to her only child, the writer, muse and political radical Nancy Cunard. They continued to correspond until his death. In one of his last letters, 15th January 1932, he confessed, 'Your letter was most welcome; I was beginning to think I had lost you – a familiar dread.' He was 80. In his Will, he left her everything, apart from two paintings.

[George Moore, Letters to Lady Cunard 1895–1933, *edited Rupert Hart-Davis, (1957).*]

John Millington Synge and Molly Allgood

In this next letter, the playwright John Millington Synge, recently turned 36, is haranguing the actress Molly Allgood (20), to whom he is secretly engaged. She is very young and tempestuous; he is highly strung and more ill than he knows with Hodgkin's lymphoma; both are recovering from the recent riots over *Playboy of the Western World*, in which Allgood starred. His illness and her profession meant that they were often apart, so he wrote to her every few days, long letters full of love and condemnation. Here he goes from berating her for imagined slights to pleading for understanding. The Irish countryside could always cheer him up and here it enables a rare moment of sensuality in the heather. As in other letters, he writes himself round to a better mood and ends movingly with a wish for the physical contact that would banish imagined fears.

GLENDALOUGH HOUSE
Monday May 27th 1907

My own dearest Love

  I got your letter this [morning], and it upsets me so much that I sat on my chair trembling all over, and I could hardly eat my breakfast. I have wired to you now to know how you are. It is a miserable business. You seem to have thought it a slight matter to tell me a lie, I, as I have often told you, and as you must see now [,] feel it very differently. We will get to understand each other better by degrees I hope and believe, so I think we need not be depressed. I don't think any good will come of discussing this affair any more in our letters. Let us drop it, and try and build our old confidence again. When I said it would be no joy to see you in London I meant merely that I was so unspeakably hurt by the way you had treated me that for the moment I had lost the joy of our love, not (I need not say), the love itself. Further, what I meant about cutting away the foundations of our happiness was, of course, that without perfect, absolute confidence and openness (that is the only thing) all sorts of misunderstandings and doubts were sure to arise, and that you had made this confidence difficult. However do not let us discuss it unless you wish to. Oh my poor love if you know how I have suffered and am suffering still. Do not talk as if you thought we should separate. How could we do it? Dont you remember those evenings when we came down from our walks so perfectly happy in each other? Isn't it some peace to you to think that we shall have that again in three or four weeks now. Dont you look forward to lying up in the heather again and eating purple grapes? My poor sweet little heart I am sorry I have hurt you, but I have been hurt as badly or worse myself so you must not blame me. I am sure that when we are together we will understand each other better, and not have these fearful troubles. It seems so simple for you to tell me straight out all that [you] are going to do, and to let us talk it over together, then we would never have any trouble, but you will not do it.

Remember I am very nervous, very highly-strung, as they call it, – if I was not I couldn't be a writer – and the only way to keep things clear is to tell me everything at the beginning, not to keep me in miserable doubt for days till I find out what has happened. My dear love we have to learn by pain and trouble how to live our life together. We both have the deep true love, I am quite sure, that will bring everything all right in the end. Do be good to me, my sweet little pet, and tell me everything as you have promised so often. I heard from Jack Yeats at last this morning. He wants me to go over at the end of this week, for a week before I go to London. I don't know whether I shall be well enough now, I am going to the doctor today. There would be no use going to Yeats if I couldn't walk about with him, and see the country. I do not know yet how I shall go it is a very troublesome journey. If I go by long sea I shall leave Dublin on Wednesday and not get to his place till Friday, but I don't think I shall go that way. Go on writing here till I send you the new address I will write to you very often of course. My knee feels very bad today I doubt that I shall be able to go at all. Perhaps I wont be able to go to London even. That would be too bad. Now promise me, my little life, that you wont worry and make yourself ill. The thought of it makes me ill too. I wonder the answer doesn't come to my wire. I hope I have read your address right it was rather hard to read what you wrote. I wrote you a long letter yesterday. It wasn't a very cheerful one I am afraid still it was better than the last. I wish I could put my two arms round you and give you a good long squeeze, and then I know we would both be all right again. Wouldn't we? Write to me cheerfully.

Your old Tramp

They eventually made public their engagement but he died in 1909, less than two years after writing this letter. Molly continued working as an actress and was successful, though not as successful as her sister, Sara, who became a Hollywood star. Molly married an English drama critic, George Mair, in 1911 and had two children. After his death in 1926 she married the Irish actor, Arthur Sinclair, but they divorced five years later. She died aged 65, her last years marred by alcoholism.

Molly Allgood

Muriel Gifford and Thomas MacDonagh

Twenty-six-year-old Muriel Gifford is writing to the prominent poet, lecturer and member of the Gaelic League, Thomas MacDonagh (34), colleague of Patrick Pearse at St Enda's progressive Irish-language school. They have just got engaged after a whirlwind courtship and are keeping it secret from their families, because she was Protestant and he Catholic. The Giffords were an unusual family – the parents and six sons were staunch unionists, but the six girls were nationalists and feminists, some of them famous. In her correspondence Muriel reveals something of the fresh, confiding, eccentric charm of Lewis Carroll's Alice – a passage in another letter in which she claims 'it is nearly impossible to write as the black kitten is sitting at the table purring at me and trying to play with my pen' could have come out of *Through the Looking Glass*. The way she gives MacDonagh's portrait a 'serious talking-to' here, about her own shortcomings, is pure Alice.

October 1911

My darling Anthony, [not her usual way of addressing him; perhaps from Shakespeare's 'Anthony and Cleopatra']

It is I – be not afraid.

I don't know why I am writing to you because I have nothing to tell you except that I love you, adore you, will marry you any time if you want – now you have the material you want for a breach of promise action.

You know I always sleep with your photograph under my pillow, darling, so that I can take it out to gaze at and kiss the first thing I wake. Well I set you up this morning & gave you a very serious talking-to about the folly of having anything to do with me – I'm afraid, my dearest, that you will be utterly disappointed with me when you get to know me better – I am not at all the ideal person you imagine – in fact I am utterly ordinary – you should have fallen in love with somebody thoroughly different – but please don't darling.

It makes me shudder when I think of the horoscope that Miss Young, or whoever it was cast for you – I imagine that you will only love me for eleven months – if it comes true, darling, don't tell me anything about it, but get a dagger or pistol & kill me before I find out anything about it. When I was lying awake this morning & thinking of you, dearest, I began to wonder why you ask me always what I love you for – & I am as far from it as ever – I love your faults – if you have any – as much as your virtues – you are generous & brave & grand my darling & I feel so proud of having won your love even if it is only for eleven months.

I laughed when I thought of your reckless generosity in getting us a box when you were probably already in debt – I love and admire that sort of thing tremendously dearest.

It was twenty to twelve when I came in last night – I expected a regular scalping – but I managed to pass if off all right – the others had all gone off to bed, & only my mother and father were up – but in the morning when I told them about it they said that I must have cast a spell on them as, just before I came in they were making an awful row about my being so late.

The dressmaker has been here today & started my dress, so I'll be able to swank on Saturday (P.G.).
Goodbye, my own darling until tomorrow

Good luck,
Muriel

They were married less than three months later on the 3rd of January 1912. This is MacDonagh writing on the eve of the wedding. He says he's happy and looking forward to their life together, but he's full of anxieties about small things – the guest list and an unspecified incident the previous night. For a poet, it's not the most passionate, candid or lyrical letter and it lacks the charm and affection of hers. Did he perhaps take Muriel for granted? Is the thought of the 'years and years' he has lost perturbing him? Having suffered a crisis in the summer of 1910 – in part over a failed love affair – he was only now emerging from a semi-reclusive existence. By the end of the letter, he's a little more romantic, thinking of her in the bath and in bed, and adding an enthusiastic post-script, which like some of his other phrases to her – 'jiggy and excited' – skirts baby-talk.

ABBOTSFORD HOTEL DUBLIN
2. J. 1912

My beloved,

Get [once?] there. I have just got back & written to [Patrick] Pearse & the Monsignor. Before I forget it, would you take charge of this thing for me? If your mother is not inviting Sherwin & Father O'Neill to lunch – do not think I want her to – she ought not ask Pearse before them. It is not that they would mind – oh – you understand. Of course it is not really necessary to write this at all, but it just struck me now that it might be unknownst to me – selfish. You see they will not have got the book or anything, and they will be there really because they are my friends. So – I told the two of them there would be no lunch or anything – as a [map?] to them – as they would prefer it so. Am I a stupid fool to write to you of this?

    And now, before I begin a new sheet – if you do not really & truly like or

145

POBLACHT NA H EIREANN.

THE PROVISIONAL GOVERNMENT
OF THE
IRISH REPUBLIC
TO THE PEOPLE OF IRELAND.

IRISHMEN AND IRISHWOMEN   In the name of God and of the dead generations from which she receives her old tradition of nationhood, Ireland, through us, summons her children to her flag and strikes for her freedom.

Having organised and trained her manhood through her secret revolutionary organisation, the Irish Republican Brotherhood, and through her open military organisations, the Irish Volunteers and the Irish Citizen Army, having patiently perfected her discipline, having resolutely waited for the right moment to reveal itself, she now seizes that moment, and, supported by her exiled children in America and by gallant allies in Europe, but relying in the first on her own strength, she strikes in full confidence of victory.

We declare the right of the people of Ireland to the ownership of Ireland, and to the unfettered control of Irish destinies, to be sovereign and indefeasible.   The long usurpation of that right by a foreign people and government has not extinguished the right, nor can it ever be extinguished except by the destruction of the Irish people.   In every generation the Irish people have asserted their right to national freedom and sovereignty, six times during the past three hundred years they have asserted it in arms.   Standing on that fundamental right and again asserting it in arms in the face of the world, we hereby proclaim the Irish Republic as a Sovereign Independent State, and we pledge our lives and the lives of our comrades-in-arms to the cause of its freedom, of its welfare, and of its exaltation among the nations.

The Irish Republic is entitled to, and hereby claims, the allegiance of every Irishman and Irishwoman.   The Republic guarantees religious and civil liberty, equal rights and equal opportunities to all its citizens, and declares its resolve to pursue the happiness and prosperity of the whole nation and of all its parts, cherishing all the children of the nation equally, and oblivious of the differences carefully fostered by an alien government, which have divided a minority from the majority in the past.

Until our arms have brought the opportune moment for the establishment of a permanent National Government, representative of the whole people of Ireland and elected by the suffrages of all her men and women, the Provisional Government, hereby constituted, will administer the civil and military affairs of the Republic in trust for the people.

We place the cause of the Irish Republic under the protection of the Most High God, Whose blessing we invoke upon our arms, and we pray that no one who serves that cause will dishonour it by cowardice, inhumanity, or rapine.   In this supreme hour the Irish nation must, by its valour and discipline and by the readiness of its children to sacrifice themselves for the common good, prove itself worthy of the august destiny to which it is called.

Signed on Behalf of the Provisional Government,

THOMAS J. CLARKE.

SEAN Mac DIARMADA,	THOMAS MacDONAGH,
P. H. PEARSE,	EAMONN CEANNT,
JAMES CONNOLLY.	JOSEPH PLUNKETT.

The 1916 Proclamation of the Irish Republic.

want lace far more than anything else – choose it not – order just the thing you want and they'll have it in a week or so.

So

The twilight long before us stretched.

It's not going to be a poem – no. My own true love, it is wonderful to think that from tomorrow you and I shall be together for ever. After all my [weakness] and casuality (!) I do feel now a little jiggy and excited – in myself – yes. I hardly know why – I have been counting the days long enough. Really this last week I have been disgusted at the delay – it is no harm to tell you now – the day I nearly broke it off with Sherwin. And now the days are ours, Miss Gifford. (By the way did the girls say anything nice about that thing last night? I was horribly depressed about it after leaving you I should have gone back – we should have waited when they called – but it never occurred to me.) What did you Bunbury* last night? There – that's over now. Tomorrow begins life for [indecipherable]. My darling, you do not know what you have brought to me and what you make me look forward to. I have lost years and years but we'll make up for that – Begad I'm getting [indecipherable]. You must be hard with me all next week, darling, and keep me straight and sober. – Are you now washing your hair or are you in bed? It is 10.20 p.m. I'm going to bed soon. Now indeed good bye good night. I'll kiss you good night in future always always. [Just?] in the old way for this one last night,

MacDonagh Limited

I'm as happy and as gay as a baby

*(*A referernce to Oscar Wilde's* The Importance of Being Earnest. *'Bunburying' refers to Muriel's habit of lying to her parents about who she was meeting when she was meeting MacDonagh.)*

Their first child was born within a year of the marriage, quickly followed by a second, but the children were soon orphaned – as a signatory to the 1916 Proclamation of the Irish Republic, MacDonagh was executed after the Easter Rising and Muriel drowned a year later off the coast of Skerries.

[NLI Gifford and MacDonagh papers, MS 44,320/3; MS 44,318 /3.]

Joseph Mary Plunkett and Grace Gifford

From Richmond Barracks, where he has just been tried by court martial for his leading part in the Easter Rising, 28-year-old consumptive Joseph Mary Plunkett writes to his fiancée, Grace Gifford, a fashionable, Slade-educated Dublin artist and cartoonist (and sister to Muriel who married another 1916 leader, Thomas MacDonagh). This is a hasty, cheerful note, scrawled on the back of Plunkett's Will (which consisted of two lines: 'I give and bequeath everything of which I am possessed or may become possessed to Grace Evelyn (Mary Vandeleur) Gifford.') The letter was delivered to Grace by a British soldier.

Richmond Barracks

RICHMOND BARRACKS
Tuesday, May 2nd, 1916

My darling child,
　　　　This is my first chance of sending you a line since we were taken. I have no notion what they intend to do with me but have heard a rumour that I am to be sent to England.
　　　　The only thing I care about is that I am not with you – everything else is cheerful. I am told that Tomas [MacDonagh] was brought in yesterday. George and Jack [Plunkett's brothers] are both here and well.

We have not had one word of news from outside since Monday 24th April except wild rumours. Listen – if I live it might be possible to get the Church to marry us by proxy – there is such a thing but it is very difficult. I am told. Father Sherwin might be able to do it. You know how I love you. That is all I have time to say. I know you love me and so I am very happy.

Your – [own or Yours ever]

Joe

MISS GRACE M. V. GIFFORD
8 TEMPLE VILLAS,
PALMERSTON RD, RATHMINES

He was right – the Church facilitated their marriage. At dawn on the 3rd of May 1916, Gifford's brother-in-law Thomas MacDonagh was executed at Kilmainham. At 6 p.m. that evening she was summoned to the gaol and taken to the prison chapel where her fiancé was led in, flanked by soldiers with bayonets. The soldiers remained while the couple was married by Fr Eugene McCarthy. Immediately afterwards Plunkett was escorted back to his cell. The next morning she was granted ten minutes conversation with her new husband; he was executed that evening. Grace lived on until 1955 as Ireland's most revered maiden widow. Granted a Civil List pension in 1932, she was buried with full military honours.

[Piaras F MacLochlainn, Last Words, Letters and Statements of the Leaders Executed After the Rising at Easter 1916 *(Cahill & Co 1971).]*

Éamonn Ceannt and Áine Ceannt

Éamonn Ceannt is writing to his wife, Áine, one hour before his execution as a leader of the Easter Rising. He is in an exalted state, his mind on God, Ireland and the nobility of his cause. He knows that Áine, his wife of ten years and an equally committed Republican and Gaelic Leaguer, will support his sacrifice. But while reflecting with satisfaction that he has politically and socially elevated his family – 'you are the wife of one of the Leaders of the Revolution' – he is briefly reminded of more intimate, 'sweeter' things, which give him the lovely image 'my sweetheart of the hawthorn hedges and summer's eves'. There is a hint of apology for perhaps excessive coldness and reserve; he assures her that he has always been proud of her, and that his 'cold exterior was but a mask'.

2.30 a.m.
8/5/16

My dearest wife Áine,

Not wife but widow when these lines reach you. I am without hope of this world and without fear, calmly awaiting the end. I have had Holy Communion and Fr. Augustine has been with me and will be back again. Dearest 'silly little Fanny.' My poor little sweetheart of – how many – years ago. Ever my comforter, God comfort you now. What can I say? I die a noble death, for Ireland's freedom. Men and women will vie with one another to shake your dear hand. Be proud of me as I am and ever was of you. My cold exterior was but a mask. It has saved me in these last days. You have a duty to me and to Rónán [their son], that is to live. My dying wishes are that you remember your state of health, work only as much as may be necessary and freely accept the little attentions which in due time will be showered upon you. You will be – you are, the wife of one of the Leaders of the Revolution. Sweeter still you are my little child, my dearest pet, my sweetheart of the hawthorn hedges and summer's eves. I remember all and I banish all that I may be strong and die bravely. I have one hour to live, then God's judgment and, through his infinite mercy, a place near your poor Grannie and my mother and father and Jem and all the fine old Irish Catholics who went through the scourge of similar misfortune from this Vale of Tears into the Promised Land. Bíodh misneach agat a stórín mo chroidhe. Tóig do cheann agus bíodh foighde agat go bhfeicimid a chéile arís i bhFlaithis Dé – tusa, mise agus Rónán beag beag bocht [sic] [Have courage, darling of my heart. Keep your head and have patience until we see each other in God's heaven – you, me and poor sweet little Ronan].

Adieu
Eamonn

He was right to foresee a prominent role for her: she spent the next decade as a leading member of Cumann na mBan and a district judge in the Sinn Féin courts. Initially anti-Treaty, she joined a peace committee working to end the civil war, and afterwards worked for the Irish White Cross. Despite Ceannt's concerns in the letter about her health, she lived a fairly long life, dying in 1954, aged 73.

[Piaras F. MacLochlainn, Last Words, Letters and Statements of the Leaders Executed after the Rising at Easter 1916 *(Cahill & Co 1971).]*

Cumann na mBan

Eric Appleby and Phyllis Kelly

English soldier, Eric Appleby, is writing from the First World War trenches to his Irish sweetheart, Phyllis Kelly, daughter of an Athlone solicitor. Both are in their early twenties, having met the previous year when he was posted to Athlone for military training. Except for five days of leave, Eric has spent all the intervening time in France; they barely know each other but he has an ardent, passionate nature and she is his succour from war. His long, loving, frequent letters seldom complain of hardship and constantly evoke their few happy times together. But in this letter he can see 'no glimmer of the end' of war, and his close friend, Burrows, has just died. He is 'utterly fed up and tired and sick of everything' but, being sensitive and selfless, his thoughts are more for the dead in combat and for the girls at home than for himself.

Monday, 11 September 1916

My darling

I got two letters today and they are both so very, very dear and wonderful that I hardly know whether I am standing on my head or my feet. They just make my Lady seem as though she was with me, if ever a letter could do that. Oh! Lady mine, why can't I be with you? When will I get back to you? Phyl, I feel nearly mad with longing for you tonight. Just all the love that I can ever feel seems to be for you, no one but you. Only this afternoon, though, Wenley was saying he thought it must be awful for those we love at home – worse than for ourselves out here. Although we out here have all sorts of little and big unpleasantness which make it like h[ell] on earth, I know it can't be as bad as what you have to go through, because we have nearly always plenty to do and life can't be so monotonous.

I've hardly sat down all day, except when I read the two dear letters. I haven't had a think for three days now. I was just dog-tired on Saturday night when

A First World War recruitment advertisement.

we got back from that race meeting, and as stiff as the dickens after the thirty-mile ride we had. Yesterday we moved again and I was like a piece of limp cotton when I turned in last night. Heaven knows what is going to happen. I'm getting now that I feel always so utterly fed up and tired and sick to death of everything. Why won't things show just a glimmer of the end, why won't they? I'm afraid, lady mine, that I'm the one that is losing all the bravery I ever had in me. Poor old Burrows's death has knocked every atom of that out of me, and I simply dread the thought of going into action again, and it's not far off. That poor girl [Burrows' Irish fiancée], the awful, terrible lonely feeling she must have in her heart now that her lover has gone. Oh! Phyl, I got such a nice letter from her, thanking me for writing and telling her so soon after it had happened. I'm going to send it to you, I think, because she said something very dear about you and I. They were going to be married as soon as he could get home; it's terribly sad. All his kit was packed up and sent to his home. I told her every little detail I could think of about his death and his grave. Please forgive my letters, but I can't help thinking about dear old Burrows's death; it makes everything so much worse out here and I keep feeling utterly miserable.

The awful longing for you comes on so very badly. What years and years it seems since that time in Athlone when you made me feel just the happiest being God ever made, at St Mark's.

Soldiers fighting in the trenches.

TUESDAY AFTERNOON

I had to stop last night and go round the lines as I was on duty yesterday and didn't get back till 12.30. Wenley and I have just got back from the new place we are going to. Oh! Lady mine, it's just awful: the dead are lying all over the place; it's a simply ghastly sight. There are Boche and our own men all mixed up – God knows why the poor devils have never been buried.

[…] No, Phyl, I'm not a wee bit tired of your telling me that you love me, why these letters you have sent me just are just the very dearest I have ever had. I can hardly believe that my Lady is longing and longing for me, and that there is just heaven on earth waiting for me when I get back.

Just all, all, all my love to you, dear heart, now and for always and always.

Your Englishman,
Eric

None of Phyllis' letters to him have survived, except the following.

Saturday, 28 October 1916

My own darling Englishman
I wonder why I'm writing this, which you may never see – oh God, perhaps even now you have gone far away from your Lady – I wonder when another telegram will come; this knowing nothing is simply terrible, I don't know what to do. I simply have sat and shivered with such an awful clutching fear at my

Soldiers loading shells in the trenches.

heart ever since your dad's wire came. It was forwarded from Athlone to Pembroke Road as that was the address we had given the post office, Mum brought it to Leeson Street. I was in my room unpacking and had just hung up 'Eric' over my bed, when the old maid came to tell me Mum was downstairs and down I rushed. That anything was the matter never occurred to me until I saw her face. Oh my love, my love, what shall I do – but I must be brave and believe all will be well – dear one, surely God won't take you from me now. It will be the end of everything that matters because, oh Englishman, you are all the world and life to me. But I must be brave like you, dear, but the words of your dad's telegram will keep ringing in my head and squashing out hope. 'Dangerously wounded'. I say it over and over again till it doesn't seem to mean anything – when I came over to Pembroke Road with Mum, I tried very hard to pray but no words will come into my head, except 'Oh God, give him back to me.' This writing to you is the only thing that makes the waiting easier – everybody is very kind, I know, but I feel I would give anything to be just by myself – I think I will go to Leeson Street now to see if there is another wire.

This letter survived because it was never sent. Three days later another telegram came from Eric's father: 'Wire just received Eric died of wounds Saturday heard nothing more.'

[Love Letters from the Front, *edited Jean Kelly (Marino Books, 2000).*]

Postcard sent home from the front, with location obliterated by the military censor.

Iseult Gonne and Ezra Pound

Twenty-four-year-old Iseult Gonne, illegitimate daughter of Maud Gonne (and passed off in public as her niece) is writing from Dublin to her lover, the modernist American poet, Ezra Pound, in London. He is married, and their brief affair is, as she suspects, already over. Her tone is poignant but witty; she tells him good gossip about the watershed 1918 Sinn Féin election and about her mother and Yeats (her 'Uncle Willie'). But underneath the worldly humour, she seems to want rescuing – 'Let's go to Spain!' – and only in French, her first language, does she achieve any intimacy.

Ezra Pound (1885-1972), Venice, Italy, 1963
© Horst Tappe / Lebrecht Music & Arts.

[8/9 December (?) 1918]

Tuesday evening

You have seen someone like me, but I, strive as I may, cannot remember the look of you; only pictorial details that are not pictures; that your eyes seem even greener than they are, that the way you walk is half like an ostrich, half like a tiger, and qui sourit comme toi? Mais purement litteraire tout ça *[and who smiles like you? But this is all too literary]*, I have lost you.

I have not since the last [4 or 11?] days gone to sleep much before 5, and been out for most of the day. At last a quiet evening! And I am falling asleep.

Wednesday

Helen has just brought me your last letter. Is America not so far as the East? To me it seems further, and I am beginning to think seriously, more perilous. I watch the papers and listen to quite sensible people's opinion, and it really looks as if Moura's [Maud Gonne] prophecy may not have been so rash after all. Danger not immediate of course, perhaps a matter of a few months, perhaps not at all; still … And I do not want you trapped in any idiotic national mess. Let's go to Spain!

No I won't get into riots. To begin with the atmosphere is not riotous at present. I went to one or two election meetings at which M. [Maud Gonne] spoke fearing there might be trouble, but all went off quite peacefully; quite entertaining in a way. Patriotism over here more absurd in its manifestations but less absurd in its essence than elsewhere; a sensuous element at least. I have been in the hills, the soil speaks. Only I wish Moura would rest; she has lost more weight and looks quite ill.

Thank god, we are moving into our house tomorrow, she will be better there than in these wretched lodgings. Meanwhile M. and W. [Maud Gonne and Yeats] are becoming the gossip of the city; they each go to their friends confiding their wrongs so that there is now the W. clan and the M. clan.

Russel [George Russell] and I are the only two who refused to take sides with this only difference that Russel says there [they are] both right and I maintain them both wrong. The climax came the day before yesterday. They met in the Green and there, among the nurses and the perambulators, proceeded to have it out finally.

M.: If only you would stop lying!

W. (gesture of arms): I have never lied, my father never told a lie, my grandfather never told a lie.

M.: You are lying now.

Delightful family! And for all my dislike of frost I earnestly wished myself at the North Pole. Perhaps I shouldn't be writing you all this rubbish and of course it is strictly entre nous *[between us]*, Uncle William's vagaries chiefly being somehow our special property.

The O'Neills and I have undertaken each other's soul; they are reading the Propertius and starting me in Plowman. Uncle W. is disappointed at my lack of appreciation of his suitor [Lennox Robinson] and rather dispises [sic] my choice of sweethearts for I am cultivating two young men – the one aged 15 the another 16. With the latter I play drafts and chess, exchange cigarettes and chocolates and kiss him solemnly on both cheeks at the door. The other is immersed in a terrific psychich [sic] chaos: cynicism throughout life the proper tendency, but death the real issue. I like those two babies; they are really my contemporaries.

Portrait of Iseult Gonne (Mrs Francis Stuart)
George William Russell, 1867-1935, Irish, 20th
century, Oil on canvas, Unframed: 56 x 46 cm
Collection, National Gallery of Ireland
Photo © National Gallery of Ireland

In fact the only person I have taken a dislike to since I am here is Lily Yeats [W.B. Yeats' sister], and it is mutual.

She is the French bourgeoisie under her worst aspects.

Mais qu'est-ce que ça fait tout ça? Et à moi, après tout, si peu! Mais est-ce que je sais ce qui t'amuse? Je ne t'ai jamais vraiment [connu] et maintenant j'ai meme oublié l'air que tu as. Je sais seulement que tu as quelquechose de très beau. Tout de meme je t'embrasse 'because it is the custom here to care for one living man' et j'aime tout ça.

[But how does all this affect you? And how does it affect me – after all, so little! But do I know what amuses you? I never really knew you and now I even forget what you look like. I only know that you have something very fine about you. All the same I embrace you 'because it is the custom here to care for one living man' and I love all that kind of thing.]

Maurice

The reference to 'cultivating two young men', perhaps to excite Pound's jealousy, is revealing in retrospect – Pound was nine years older than her and she had refused a proposal from Yeats, who was in his fifties, and from the 30-year-old playwright, Lennox Robinson, but eighteen months after writing this letter she married a 17-year-old boy, the future writer Francis Stuart.

Pound later referred affectionately to Iseult as 'a great dear with a sense of humour, 6 ft 2 I think. And no one else so appreciated the spectacle of Unc Wm/ as we two from the Non-prix Nobel angles', but the love of his life was the American violinist, Olga Rudge, whom he met in the 1920s.

Olga Rudge

Francis Stuart Francis Stuart - In his house, in Dublin (detail), 1983. Irish novelist 1902–2000
© T.Martinot / Lebrecht Music & Arts.

There is a curious parallel between Pound's fate and Francis Stuart's: both were incarcerated after the Second World War for alleged fascist sympathies (although Stuart, as the citizen of a neutral country, was not held long). Stuart's marriage to Iseult had broken down before he left for Germany in 1939. She lived on quietly in Wicklow with their two children and died in 1954, her obvious potential as a writer largely unrealised.

[Letters to W.B. Yeats and Ezra Pound from Iseult Gonne, edited by A. Norman Jeffares, Anna MacBride White and Christina Bridgwater, Palgrave, 2004.]

Peadar Kearney and Eva Kearney

Thirty-seven-year-old Peadar Kearney, Gaelic Leaguer, 1916 veteran and author of the national anthem, is writing to his wife, Eva, from Ballykinlar internment camp in County Down, where he had been interned almost a year for his part in the War of Independence. His tone in letters home can be querulous – he admonishes her if letters come late and reminds her sharply that 'if it's hard on you, it's 10,000 times harder on me' – and he is generally more interested in practicalities, like food parcels, than he is loving, but this letter, written on a lovely morning when he's in a rare good mood, is more intimate, and reminds us why it was hard to write of love from the camp – the letters were of course censored.

FROM P KEARNEY 457
HUT 28 COB. CAMP 1
BALLYKINLAR
Sunday, Sept. 4th 1921

Dear Eva,

This is a lovely morning such as you can only get in this country in September. (We remember we're in Ireland when we see the mountains & wooded country beyond the barbed wire.) As the Englishman says I am feeling 'good' and can't complain. I hope you and the lads and the weather are as 'good' up there on Ceannis Fort.

I got parcel & letter yesterday all complete. You 'copped' the idea of list at last when you pasted it on tea. Stick another bottom of box youre right. Putting them in loose was useless. Everything is opened except condensed milk, butter generally has the appearance of having gone thro a bayonet charge & the salt you sent was emptied clean out amongst the other articles in parcel before last. Don't send any more tea till I ask for it. Butter always. Send packets of safety matches. If I start making beads, copper wire will do, other wire useless. The pipe is the business. Put in a hanker or two. You made my mouth water with the picture you drew of the house on the hill. You remember McCalls song 'oh bitter my woe I must go to some far distant part, oer the foam I must roam from my home & the wife of my heart. From the children I love, God above! must I bow to Thy will. Then once more 'ere I go, slan Beo! to the house on the hill.' I dont think I have it right, but anyhow youll remember. A day like this the situation is grand for I know the country well. As the Irish poet says 'If I were standing once more in the midst of my people old age would fall from me & I'd be young again'. However I'm in a very good humour with myself & everyone else because your news has been a great relief to me, proving that the real anxiety here is not for oneself but those you love. I'd like to write a good 'wicked' letter to you but as other people might be shocked you must only fancy that my arms are round you and that Im whispering to you, rather poor satisfaction, but there's nothing else for it.

GRAY
MCMLXI

Brendan Behan

Peadar was released on parole a few months later, just before the Anglo-Irish treaty of December 1921. He took the pro-Treaty side and after the civil war, retired from politics, returning to house painting, the family trade shared by his nephews, Brendan and Dominic Behan. He died at home in Inchicore, in relative poverty in 1942, the same year his nephew Brendan was convicted of IRA activity and sent to Mountjoy Prison.

[My dear Eva, letters from Ballykinlar Internment Camp, introduced by Seamus de Burca, Litho Press 1976.]

Harry Boland, Kitty Kiernan and Michael Collins

On the eve of his departure to America on revolutionary business, Harry Boland is begging his sweetheart, Kitty Kiernan, to marry him. He has causes for concern – he'll be away six months, she's having doubts and they are in the midst of a 'love triangle' with his best friend, Michael Collins – but Boland's innate optimism and cheerfulness chase his fears. He looks forward to their honeymoon in California and he never threatens – 'no matter what manner our Triangle may work out', they will remain friends. All three are around 30 years old, and life seems long. The image Boland signs off with – 'lips of my heart' – may be clumsy but it is certainly lover-like; his heart – mentioned four times in the letter – is engaged.

QUEEN'S HOTEL, CORK
1 October 1921

Pulse of my heart,

I'm here in Cork and feel just as sad and lonely as the day itself, and God knows this is a real Cork day, raining soft and persistent!

I'm wondering if you are ever a wee bit lonely for me; and are you longing as I am for the day when we shall meet again? R.S.V.P.

How I can leave you even at the order of 'the Chief' I do not know, and I'm asking myself all the time if I have not made a great mistake in leaving you behind. Won't you send me a wireless to the Celtic and say you have made up your mind. If you have done so, cable Yes, and if you're still in doubt, then for God's sake try to make up your mind, and agree to come with me.

You will know by now that we have agreed to the Conference, but what may come of it I cannot say. We will know very soon if it is to be Peace or War. If Peace, I will be home in about six months. If war, I shall be in America until Dáil Éireann replaces me, and I would just love to have you come to America where we will spend our honeymoon in perfect bliss!

Mick and I spent the last night together. He saw me home at 2 a.m., and as I had to catch the 7.35 a.m. I bade him goodbye – only to find him at Kingsbridge as fresh as a daisy to see me off. I need not say to you how much I love him, and I know he has a warm spot in his heart for me, and I feel sure in no matter what manner our Triangle may work out, he and I shall be always friends.

I go to Cove in a few hours, and soon I shall feel the tang of the Western Ocean and open my lungs to its wonderful ozone. I am going back for the final phase of our work, and all the time I shall carry you with me in my heart, and now I want you to send me a little photo of yourself, one that I can carry in my match or cigarette case. Have a good long chat with Father Shanley, and do come back with him and marry me, after which we shall go to California for our honeymoon.

I have now to meet a gang of Corkonians who expect me to call on them ere I leave the Rebel City. So I bid you a fond farewell and, as I can not kiss you with my lips, I do so a million times with the lips of my heart.
May God bless and guard you,

Your devoted lover,
Harry

Michael Collins and Kitty Kiernan

On the 14th of October Harry was still writing to Kitty from New York of his great hope, and he even got his mother to write, but Kitty had made up her mind about the 'Triangle' and was entering into a long, fraught correspondence with Michael Collins, who was less open, lover-like and committed than Boland. In this uncharacteristically lengthy letter, he is uncharacteristically lyrical – the refrain 'you were not forgotten' recalls early Gaelic poetry – but characteristically defensive and elusive.

He throws her accusation of lack of commitment back at her, suggesting that she, not him, will wish to 'get out of it'. His opening and closing salutes are business-like compared to Harry's; he puts her off trying to meet him, admits the possibility of failure in their romance and is petulant about her nagging when he's under such strain. There is no talk of honeymoons in the sun or of his heart – it is not an altogether reassuring letter, but this is as passionate as he got with her in print.

Harry Boland

LONDON

20 October 1921

Kitty, dear,

This is to answer yours of Monday evening. I have a kind of idea that I ought really return that letter and let you look at it, and compare it with this reply, for I'll try this time to reply solidly to all your points. But, first of all, don't be putting up too severe tests. Don't attempt to walk before we have learnt to crawl. That is a fatal mistake. It is something that can't be done.

By the bye first of all – do you know how your letter strikes me, I mean in net substance? It is this, that you are trying to get out of it. Is this really so? I don't want to get out of it. I want it to work out and I promise to do my part of it. If it's not possible, then God help us, but let us have a fair chance. Isn't that right? Last night H [Helen, Kitty's sister] asked me if she could do anything for us. I said no — we have to get this thing settled ourselves. Isn't that right also?

You were not forgotten, and if my letter had not reached you at all, you should know that you were not forgotten, and if I were in jail and couldn't write to you at all, you should also know that you were not forgotten. I know I wasn't and that in spite of your not writing – actually not writing – for two days; and, if you only knew the difficulty in finding time, you'd know how unfair you were to talk of long letters. (Since I commenced this, I have had to deal with several business letters, a few callers and a few phone calls.) I don't find it difficult to write you a long letter – I want to write to you all day really – but I have many obligations, and don't forget that, even in the midst of them, I didn't let two days pass without writing. But I musn't mind, must I? However, perhaps I do mind. And I'm not going to be cross any more, and that's that, and I'm not in good form any longer, and I wasn't able to get to bed until 3 o'c this morning, and I was up at 7.15 to go to the Oratory, and that's that, and I'm sorry if I may be appearing to be unpleasant to you. And it's my real friends that have to suffer these things, and please don't you blame me.

Don't be disappointed about the other thing. I don't want to be a hypocrite about it or anything else. I'm getting into that direction. Will you leave it at that for the moment?

[…] Will you really come here? Very likely you would not see too much of me. Don't you think that the seeing part of it has gone a good deal deeper now? I regard your attitude as being correct. If the contract be entered into, it is only just that the terms shall be kept. Isn't that right? I do understand you – whatever else you make a mistake about, don't make any mistake about that. And perhaps it is you who would feel different next year, and haven't we to chance that too? And if you really think I don't consider these things, and if you really do trust such a thing lightly, then you know nothing about me.

And in spite of it, I would not change a word in your letter for I don't like gramophone effects. I like people to say what they themselves think and mean.

Were we really criticized? And by whom? So much the worst for the critics! Don't mind them. That was the thing – we ought to have been away from everybody. When we were, there was no necessity for criticism. Isn't that right also? By the bye, do you really think I'd laugh over it now? Were my explanations so utterly bad? You need not dread our next meeting.

I look forward to it more eagerly than ever before. And, finally, you are right – If it can't last through misfortune and trouble and difficulty and unpleasantness and age then it's no use. In riches and beauty and pleasure it is so easy to be quite all right. That is no test though.

> Goodbye Kit and every good wish for the day,
>
> *M.*

Look at the enclosed. Please destroy it as it may be regarded as a breach of confidence. It is not though, really.

> Yours,
>
> M

Kitty continued to agitate. In this histrionic *tour-de-force*, written six weeks after the above letter, she minutely dissects her feelings, projects into a cosy future, begs him to confide in her, and makes a daring reference to wishing to tire him sexually. She reflects that he loves her 'as well as any of the others I had thought of marrying' (not better!), but clearly there are problems over his failure to name a date for their wedding. She has made scenes about this, demanding 'something definite', but now she gives up the attack, claiming to be 'happy to drift and drift as long as I know you love me'. Kitty was an orphan – a parent would presumably have stopped Collins' tendency to drift. This is, as she herself writes, 'some letter', but she certainly picked her moments: the date is early December 1921. Collins was in London negotiating the Anglo-Irish Treaty.

The first Dáil - 1920.

Michael Collins

Kitty (in black, seated beside the priest) at her sister Maud's wedding.

[c.1st December 1921]

My very dear Michael,

When I awoke this morning, the first thing I thought of was the letter I wrote last night. It was still lying on the table. It was a silly letter I know, but I decided to post it (11 o'clock post) as I have never been sorry for anything I wrote to you, no matter how silly and stupid it appeared afterwards. I was doubly glad today, when your long letter came, that I had sent it. I like your letter very much and it made me full of resolutions. I really probably misunderstood you. You asked me if I recalled the letter you wrote one night very late in Dublin.

You might not ask. I recall only too well all our little episodes before you went to London.

The connection with Dublin and you I look back on with the greatest happiness, and I delight to think about it. I 'seem' to have had no worries then, no thought of anything, but just lived for the day. Perhaps it was that I had not the same feeling for you then as I have now. (I hope you were not thinking at me in your letter when you remarked that you don't like demonstrative people. I quite agree, and hate it in public, and sometimes you must get fed up with me telling you about the change I feel so keenly that has come over me. When I cease to be surprised shortly it should be more comfortable for you. But you will forgive me just once more for boring you about it.) Then I was easily pleased and quite happy. I felt you liked me, that you were sure about it, and I didn't worry, and very sensible too. But I found that I grew to love you more and more each day, and then the worries began. I thought if you discovered this you might cool off and I tried to be a bit elusive, but then it became too serious, far too serious to my mind to hide it and I let you know 'in every way'. But all the same I wasn't brave enough. I was afraid. Every day the feeling grew stronger and with it the fear, because I had always a feeling that if I ever thought anyone wants it, I'd be very very keen, not realising at first that you might be the one (poor you). It came on gradually (ah, you did it, 'you knew the way'! like the song). Anyway I then realised how serious it was for both of us and, of course, I got all the more anxious to make you happy. But I had also the feeling that I wanted you to be free absolutely to change if you wished, and that's why, and I'm sure you may have misunderstood me often. I gave you so many chances just because I liked you. [...] I fought it successfully for a short time, then I decided, if it is a question of marriage (two nights before Helen's wedding on the stairs and the night following it, when you really wanted me) why not marry the one I really love, and what a cowardly thing of me to be afraid to marry the one I really want, and who loves me just as well as any of the others I had thought of marrying.

Then London came. I should not have gone. It gave rise to such talk. People got to know about it, and I thought it better from a girl's very conventional and narrow point of view that we better have something definite, and so we have drifted. *Please*, sweetheart, *don't* misunderstand me now. I can't explain. It is only I felt, if we were ever to part, it would be easier for us both, especially for me, to do it soon, because later it would be bitter for me. But I'd love you just the same, even if we both *or you* decided on it.

Now don't think by this that I want a row or want you to end it. Not likely. I want you only not to think bad of me when we had those scenes. Testing you! With the feeling as a girl – 'better have it now than later'. If you were me you would see it clearly too. Don't think I want you to decide definitely now. I am happy to drift and drift as long as I know you love and we will be one day together. I fancy sometimes – as girls do – a little nest you and I, two comfy chairs, a fire, and two books (now I'm not too ambitious) and no worries. You feeling perfectly free, as if not married, and I likewise. I'd on believe, as you used to say, 'it will be a great arrangement.' I will promise you when we feel perfectly confident – as I have now for ages – I'll have no more rows. Truly if I didn't love you so well I wouldn't want your love so badly. I always picture – do you like my picture? – myself sitting on your knee – not the two big chairs so often – until I tire you. Cruel isn't it? We will, won't we, be real lovers? Say we will. You don't trust me or answer my important questions. And as the one I have a dim recollection of, if you liked me to love you so much or if it was a nonsense, can't you tell me all your worries? If you can't have me as a friend [who is] ready to do anything for you (almost?), who could you trust?

This must finish now and it's some letter. You couldn't bring yourself to write this sort of thing, the famous M.C. All I wish now is that it please you, gives you some sunshine, and helps to make the day easy for you. That will always be my ambition. With that we should have no worry.

Believe me, your own little pet, friend, and everything,
Kit.

I have heaps more to write, but the post goes now. Excuse writing. In haste.
K.

Micheal Collins

Collins replied to this outpouring with the careless aside: 'No, I do not take up that challenge about the letters'. In January he did announce their engagement to the Dáil – but only because he was forced into it by Constance Markiewicz's bizarre suggestion that he was about to marry the Princess Mary. Kitty tried to set a June date for their wedding – 'Now I have proposed to you'. But she had no luck: in June the civil war broke out. On the 31st of July 1922 Harry Boland was killed; followed, exactly three weeks later, by Collins. In 1925 Kitty married a Civil War veteran, Felix Cronin. They had two sons, one called Michael Collins Cronin. The marriage was unhappy.

[In Great Haste, the Letters of Michael Collins and Kitty Kiernan, *edited Leon O Broin, Gill and Macmillan, 1983.*]

Kitty Kiernan

Micheal Collins was ambushed and killed in August 1922.

Liam O'Flaherty and Kitty Tailer

'O my America, my Newfoundland!' – John Donne's joyful exclamation to his mistress hovers over this letter from Liam O'Flaherty to his new girlfriend, Kitty Tailer. It is 1937 and the 41-year-old O'Flaherty is famous for his socialism; for his novel, *The Informer*, filmed by John Ford; and as the embodiment of a certain kind of hard-drinking, horse-betting, very handsome and rugged West-of-Irelander. Many of his best stories were set in his native Aran Islands. In 1924 he had caused a scandal in Dublin by running off with Margaret Barrington, the wife of a TCD history professor, Edward Curtis. They weren't happy. Ten years later he met Kitty Tailer, an American, freshly divorced with two sons. Judging by this enthusiastic letter, she represented the vitality, wealth and happiness of America, compared to Irish misery and poverty. He has recently given up drinking alcohol for her and is prepared for anything, including abandoning literature for Hollywood ...

[HEADED PAPER OF HOTEL LUTÉTIA, 43 BOULEVARD RASPAIL, PARIS]
Wednesday night p.m. Paris 26 March 1937

Darling Sweetie Pie,

I am on my way back from Dublin – bound for Paris. Dublin was too frightfully melancholy, and I just didn't feel there was any point to staying there. A kind of slime was seeping through the streets, it drizzled, the people looked miserably poor, impolite, unhappy. The influence of Catholic Fascism was everywhere, and I had the feeling of being in a dead city. Maybe it was the sudden change from the terrific vitality and the wealth of New York, but there it is. At the moment I am determined to apply for citizenship in U.S.A. and settle down in the west. 'How long will this last?' says Kitty.

Oh darling, I love you so! I am exhausted with sleepless travelling and I am only half conscious, but I am aware that you are now my whole life and that I would be utterly lost without you. I

got your lovely telegram in London. Aren't I lucky that you love me in return, because I am too fond of you

to live without you.

I shouldn't write now as I am silly for lack of sleep. I couldn't sleep on the Normandie on account of the nervous exhaustion of listening to politics at meals and in the smoking room all day […] Otherwise it was not a bad crossing, though dull and dreary, since I was going from you instead of coming to you like last time. I think we had better get a divorce for me in Reno and get married and live on the American Continent, than run back and forth like this, don't you?

[…] It's going to be awfully long until you come but I shall put up with it better than last year, because I feel better in mind now that I am a sober man and we are nearer to one another.

[…] Didn't hear much about *Famine* [his new novel] in either London or Dublin, but I had the feeling it did not raise a tidal wave in either the Thames or Liffey. I don't think any thing could. Perhaps Hollywood has, after all, taken the place of literature in the human mind. If so let's get in on it. There's no point in struggling against fact, is there, sweet?

This letter, duck, is mad and pertains somewhat to the outpourings of an *énergumène* [fanatic]. However! I am full of love and yearning for you, little darling and I am enthusiastic, optimistic and *enfoutiste* [don't give a damn].

[…] Well, sweet one, I'll write a few words again with that article the day after tomorrow.

Love, love, love
Pidge

They never got married, nor stopped 'running back and forth', and he never emigrated – but they were together until his death in 1984, though they often lived apart, she in America and he in Dublin. His later years were not as successful or productive as his earlier ones but Kitty remained his comfort. In a letter the day after his 76th birthday, he wrote:

I feel overwhelmed with tenderness, because of your unfading and unmerited kindness towards this hapless *Barbare des Iles* … How strange it is that the human animal, so coarse and unfeeling and even brutal, can be able to join so totally with another life that was originally alien, totally alien and unknown.

[The Letters of Liam O'Flaherty, edited by A.A. Kelly (Wolfhound Press, 1996).]

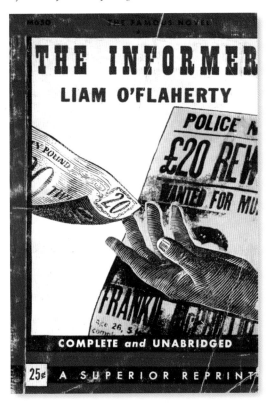

Early paperback cover of The Informer

Iris Murdoch and Frank Thompson

Dame (Jean) Iris Murdoch by Tom Phillips, oil on canvas, 1984–1986, detail. © National Portrait Gallery, London.

From the London Blitz, the future novelist Iris Murdoch pours her heart out in a ten-page letter to her friend Frank Thompson, an army captain serving in the Middle East. Both are in their early twenties and he has been smitten with her since their first meeting at Oxford, when he wrote to a friend, 'I've met my dream-girl – a poetic Irish Communist who's doing Honour Mods. I adore her'. Iris had many suitors, was independent and free-thinking, and wouldn't commit, but she termed the artistic and polyglot Frank 'the most remarkable person that I met as an undergraduate'. Their war correspondence, initiated in 1941 when he was first posted abroad, developed their intimacy. In this letter she has some important news to impart: the loss of her virginity. The worldly, dispassionate, bravely nonchalant (but awkward) tone is typical of young, free-thinking intellectuals. She later judged these letters, 'very affectionate but a bit stilted, young person's letters'.

5, SEAFORTH PLACE, LONDON
23 January 1943

Darling, the mice have been eating your letters again … [I don't mind] how many dangers you face, so long as I don't know at the time, & you emerge in good condition and don't suffer miseries en route of course … [I am] hellishly lonely [despite being in] great and beautiful and exciting London. I should tell you that I have parted company with my virginity. This I regard in every way as a good thing. I feel calmer & freer – relieved from something which was obsessing me, & made free of a new field of experience. There have been two men. I don't think I love either of them – but I like them & I know that no damage has been done. I wonder how you react to this – if at all? Don't be angry with me – deep down in your heart.(I know you are far too Emancipated to be angry on the surface.) I am not just going wild. In spite of a certain amount of wild talk I still live my life with deliberation.

Frank Thompson

The letter took twelve weeks to reach Frank. He replied immediately with a complicated letter, ostensibly disclaiming anger but manifesting it through a few hurtful, even threatening comments; he insinuates that she was in danger of becoming frigid but also that the men she sleeps with hate her. He is sarcastic on the subject of those men; she was right to fear what was going on below the surface. But her frankness did call out a revelation of his own – that he suffers from the classic Madonna-Whore complex with regard to women. By the end of the letter, his usual gentle disposition has reasserted itself.

[LEVANT]
22 April 1943

I could have no cause for anger. Nor can I, since I am not conventional after the modern fashion, be unreservedly glad without due reflection ... I know of course that your men are not ordinary men but parfit gentle knights. But it will take years of sorrow to realise how violently misogynistic men are *au fond* ... a theory which I'm still engaged in formulating ... I, you see, have messed up my sex-life ... [with] a most terrible dichotomy by which women fall into two categories – Women it would be rather nice to sleep with provided one didn't have to talk with them for more than five minutes / women one really likes *avec lesquelles il ne vaut pas s'embeter dans un lit* [with whom it's not worth bothering in bed] … To medicine me from this would probably take years of psychotherapy combined with the best type of free love … But having suffered all this, I am coming to the conclusion that it is better to abstain altogether until one falls head over heels in love … I remember thinking … often … that a good love-affair would do you the devil a lot of good. [I feared you were wedded to] a cold virginity from which it would be yearly more difficult to free yourself. So, on balance, it is obviously a subject for joy. If I've said anything here that is clumsy or stupid, forgive me. I'm afraid there is no finesse about me, Irushka … Do write me more long letters like your last. I talk a lot of baloney when I answer, but maybe I understand more than I let on.

Iris responded with more worldly posturing but was evidently a little perturbed by his letter and wondered if they should stop 'prying into each other's minds':

As a matter of interest, how have you fared with women in the East? I don't mean from the grand passion point of view, but just from the sex experience point of view […] Do you spend your days lying with lovely Iranians? How do you feel about that racket now? It's terrible, Frank, how little we know really in spite of fairly frequent letters of how the other party is developing in these fast and fatal years. Perhaps we shouldn't pry into each other's minds … God what a difference half an hour's conversation would make.

They continued in this worldly, dispassionate vein, probably not addressing their true feelings. On the 21st of April 1944 he wrote her, 'I can honestly say I've never been in love. When I pined for you I was too young to know what I was doing – no offence meant.' By this stage she was interested enough to write him a love poem (never sent) and to go out with his best friend. Who knows how it would have ended? On the 31st of May 1944 Frank's unit was captured in Bulgaria and he was executed a week later. Iris took more lovers – one of them, the Nobel Prize winner Elias Canetti, certainly came to hate her, as Frank had warned. She always planned to put off marriage until she was 35 – Frank was her first choice, but, denied him, she married (at 37) John Bayley, who proved an excellent husband, eventually nursing her through Alzheimer's. Frank haunted her prize-winning fiction and her dreams, though not as much as Canetti, who was her principal muse.

[Peter Conradi, Iris Murdoch, a Life (2001).]

Dame (Jean) Iris Murdoch by Tom Phillips,
oil on canvas, 1984–1986
© National Portrait Gallery, London.

Erwin Schrödinger and Sheila May Greene

Austrian anti-Nazi refugee and Nobel-winning scientist Erwin Schrödinger (57) is explaining his philosophy of life and sex to his much younger girlfriend, the (married) Irish actress and political activist, Sheila May Greene, a protegée of Micheál Mac Liammóir at the Gate Theatre. Sheila was in addition to the ménage à trois Schrödinger already enjoyed with his wife and girlfriend, but then, as he explains here, he hated to go to bed alone. His domestic arrangements had proved too immoral for Harvard and Oxford, but did not deter Eamon de Valera from inviting the discoverer of 'wave mechanics' to Ireland to help establish the Dublin Institute for Advanced Studies.

August 1944

Sheila, please do not think I am a complicated man for whom his so-called 'brain work' plays a prominent role in itself and is linked with his natural life by most involved, curved, branched channels. No. They are neighbours. Both are equally simple and straightforward, equally natural. I have never been able to understand, let alone explain, anything difficult or mysterious or involved. I hate it.

The simplest thing in the world is to go to bed. We have to do it every day. And everybody hates to do it alone. And you have given me more, more, a thousand times more than anybody else ever has: your clear, clean, simple, straightforward love. Not for one second has there ever been any petty play about it, nor will there ever be.

Within days or weeks of writing this, Schrödinger was suggesting that their affair, which he had first presented as a mystical union, was merely sexual and ephemeral. Sheila replied with this remarkable letter, which seems to speak for all women who discover the man is only interested in sex. In an oblique or unconscious reference to Schrödinger's most famous theoretical experiment, she compares his love for her to her own for her cat.

[Mid-August 1944]

I looked into your eyes and found all life there, that spirit which you said was no more you or me, but us, one mind one being, one loving. For two months that common soul existed. Today I saw the scales creep over your eyes and I watched it die. It slipped away without even a struggle. My mind went numb, there was nothing I could do, or ever can do, to give us that again — You love me still, I know. I love my cat because he's soft and sweet and lets me play with him. You can love with tenderness, with devotion, you can love me all your life, but we are two now, not one. Why did you let it go? Wasn't it worth fighting for? My fault maybe in the beginning, for I am thoughtless and foolish, but surely age and learning bring some sort of wisdom to a man … Don't you know that anything could be achieved when you and I are together, that even though I am young and scatter-brained, when you open your mind to me, I can see with it and use it. But no, you talk of one lover placing the other on too high a pedestal. You talk of loving, but perhaps not

approving. In a few brief sentences you kill the greatest thing I ever had, and then you ask me into bed, unless I would prefer to go out for a drink. Of course, in bed we're all right, we'll always do that well. But what is gone, will it ever, ever come again? I could stand deliberate cruelty from you and I wouldn't really mind, but the heart-breaking thing is that you didn't even know what you were doing. I can only pray that our child has been conceived a week ago, or two.

Her prayers were answered; she was pregnant and gave birth to Schrödinger's daughter in 1945. Since her marriage was barren, a child was perhaps what she wanted most from the affair. Her husband, the brilliant Celtic scholar David Greene, knew he wasn't the father but acknowledged the child and took custody when they divorced. Schrödinger, a life-long consumptive, retired home to Vienna in 1957 and died four years later, aged 73. His name survives on a crater at the far side of the moon.

[*Walter Moore*, Schrödinger, Life and Thought, *1989.*]

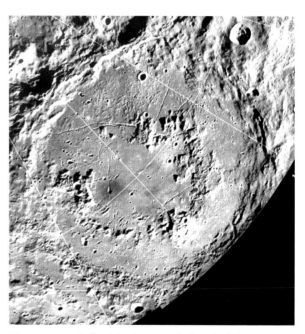

The crater named after Schrödinger, on the far side of the Moon.
NASA

Patrick Kavanagh and Hilda Moriarty

The 40-year-old poet is writing to the great unrequited love of his life to tell her that he is no longer in love with her. Hilda Moriarty was a stunning 22-year old medical student when Kavanagh developed an obsession with her, stalking her around Dublin and even to her family home in Dingle. He was, as he writes here, literally 'mad' about her, and in this wry witty letter is so relieved to have put the madness behind him that he cheerfully kills her off.

62 PEMBROKE ROAD
31 May 1945

My dearest Hilda,
Please do not take exception to the address of 'dearest' or think it a presumption on my part. I am no longer mad about you although I do like you very very much. I like you because of your enchanting selfishness and I really am your friend – if you will let me.

I should not, perhaps, write this letter to you without you replying to my other, but I am in such a good humour regarding you that I want you to know it. Remembering you is like remembering some dear one who has died. There has never been – and never will be – another woman who can be the same to me as you have been. Your friendship & love or whatever it was, was so curious, so different.

Write to me a friendly letter even if I cannot see you. I met Cyril in the Country Shop and he was looking well.
Believe me, Hilda,
Yours fondly,

Patrick

Patrick Joseph Kavanagh, by Patrick Swift, lithograph, 1956
© *estate of Patrick Swift / National Portrait Gallery, London.*

He was right that there would 'never be another woman who can be the same to me as you have been'; she was the inspiration behind 'Raglan Road'. The brief contrast he makes in this letter between her 'enchanting selfishness' and her inspirational qualities find fuller expression in that ballad, which metamorphoses Kavanagh from spurned stalker to angel, and reduces Hilda to clay. She married a tall flamboyant Limerick engineering student, Donogh O'Malley, who went on to a brilliant political career with Fianna Fáil (he, Charles Haughey and Brian Lenihan were known in the 1960s as the Three Musketeers). Kavanagh waited until his sixties to finally marry his girlfriend of seven years, Katherine Moloney, but he died seven months later, on the 30th of November 1967, three months before Donogh O'Malley.

[NLI, MS 46, 868r]

John Ford and Maureen O'Hara

On his way to Ireland to prepare for filming *The Quiet Man,* legendary director John Ford (56) is writing (from the plane) to his stunning red-haired leading lady, Maureen O'Hara. Addressing her as 'Herself', he protests his love and devotion, which he intertwines with his emigrant's love for Ireland. O'Hara, twenty-six years old and on her second husband, was astonished to receive this letter – she was close friends with Ford, whom she called 'Pappy', and with his wife, Mary; her daughter played with their grandchildren.

Maureen O'Hara

November 19, 1950

[To 'Herself']
En route to Eire (again)
       All rite! All rite! All rite!
       So American Air service is
better! I always said you were smarter
than me – My only casualty was y'da's
pencil – (Charlie Fitz's Xmas pencil – don't make any wise cracks) It got bent
like pretzel (y'da's pencil I mean).
       You know-agra-being Irish & fey – (did y'not know I was Irish? I am –
from good Spiddal stock – good solid peasant shopkeeper stock). And as I was
saying, being Irish & fey … I had a hunch about our trips-you-west-me east.
       An' thank God it happened to me for if anything happened to you – I
would die. For I love you so much my darling – a million words couldn't tell –
and them in Gaelic –
       It's twenty-two hours now since I saw you & my heart is breaking

already – but again it swells & mends when I think of you – not your beauty-intelligence-talent or even your lovely eyes – but for you as a person.

I worship you – for yourself.

Believe me! My love –

(we are flying over Palm Springs – and I kissed you!)

Do you like Honolulu? It's nice but not for us –

I hope Elmer & the boys played sweetly for you. The sun smiled on you & that palm leaves waved at you as you drove to the Royal and that you found this note when you got there –

(Which is higher – O'Connell Bridge or the Cliffs of Moher?) Arrah Maisín ma chree how much happiness you have given me & how little I've given you – but girleen I love you so much –

As this letter might go astray I won't sign except as Seán Aloysius O'Feeney John Ford.

Who claims he's your fella –

'I see in you perfected-All that's wrong in Me'.

Maureen claims she dismissed this letter as drunken nonsense, and didn't give it another thought, but she did write to him shortly afterwards from location in Australia, telling him how unpleasant the shoot was and how much she missed him, 'Oh Pappy, we'd be so thrilled to look up and see you walking down the avenue'. This had a (surely predictable?) effect; more letters started arriving – 'Oh Maisín agrad, why can't we just chuck it and go back to our lovely Isle? Life is so different there – the people-our people-are nicer. We can social climb a bit and say we're peasants'. In June of 1951 she arrived in Ireland to begin filming *The Quiet Man*. Ford behaved no different to how he had always been and never mentioned the letters, but in later life he continued to obsess over her, asking her to run away with him. She insisted that he was only ever in love with an image, and in her autobiography her interpretation of the letters is that he was 'actually living the *Quiet Man* story while creating it ... That crazy, brilliant, old son of a bitch [was] still writing his script ... They [weren't] love letters from John Ford to Maureen O'Hara [but] from Sean Thornton to Mary Kate Danaher [characters in *The Quiet Man*]'. She denied ever having an affair with him, but although she married three times she called her autbiography *'Tis Herself* – after Ford's name for her in the love letters.

*Film-maker John Ford on set of the film
Seven Women in 1965, Mary Evans.*

Elizabeth Bowen and Charles Ritchie

Elizabeth Bowen by Bassano
half-plate film negative, 25 July 1939
© *National Portrait Gallery, London*

From her ancestral home, Bowen's Court in Cork, Elizabeth Bowen (57) is using all her novelist's arts to keep her younger lover, the Canadian diplomat Charles Ritchie (50). Their affair started in London in 1941 when she was a married literary celebrity, author of *The Last September* and *The Death of the Heart*, and he was a bachelor-about-town attached to the Canadian High Commissioner. In the sixteen years since, he has married his second cousin and Bowen has been widowed, but their affair has continued, fed by letters and occasional meetings. In her biographer's words: 'Though they were never under the same roof for more than a week, they were never parted emotionally'. This letter is highly literary; not only does Bowen compare their affair to an absorbing book, but the scene she paints of the man and woman driving could be out of a novel: being 'sucked on and on' through a long tunnel of trees, feeling 'the curious compulsive smoothness of the car'. It is – surely intentionally – sexual. Her bitchiness about Ritchie's wife, Sylvia, is characteristic.

Bowen's Court, Saturday, 23rd March 1957

My dearest – I got and loved your two postcards from Munich: they are so very beautiful. I am keeping them on the library chimney-piece …

I think it's partly a sort of loneliness of mind – as though a book one was completely absorbed in and utterly riveted to had suddenly (even though only temporarily) been snatched from one. I mean, our continuous talking, when we are together, is like that. And in a way what we talk about weaves itself into a story. What happens next? I am always wanting to know. Even small practical things, each other's quite passing preoccupations, are so interesting, exciting. And when we have to part, all those small stories are suspended. Also I miss knowing what is in your mind.

Do you know, one of the things I remember most, I mean dwell on most, about last time you were here was the end of the drive home from Kerry … It was the last part of the road coming into Mallow from the Killarney side, being sucked – as it almost felt like – on and on under that long tunnel of trees in the darkening twilight. You were talking about the little girls and girls of your childhood and late-adolescent days in Halifax, and the different kinds of feeling you had for them. Really it was a conversation about love, not in the abstract but as applied to people, the different kinds of love aroused by different kinds of people – and particularly the sharpness and bafflingness of that when one is young. The mood of the evening, with that faint taste of spring about it, and the curious compulsive smoothness of the car – I felt as though someone else, not me, were driving – all seemed to melt into what you were saying. And my love for you reached a pitch of anguish, almost, out of our very nearness and sheer happiness. Those particular miles of tree-road will always be yours. In a way I don't want to drive them again till you come back, though I suppose I shall […]

How is Sylvia [Ritchie's wife] since she came back? I always wonder whether she ever varies or is always the same. This is not unkindness, merely the speculation one cannot but feel about any human being. Some things must make dents in her, surely, though I must say in my limited experience I have never seen anything do so …

Wouldn't it be lovely if you had a tape-recorder machine and could talk to me on it? But that would mean some outside person (I suppose) would have to read the tape off, and type what was on it. Oh Charles I feel so physically low and shivery: I think I'm on the verge of getting a ghastly cold. I shall go to bed very early tonight with 2 hot water bottles.

I love you.
Elizabeth

None of his letters to her have survived, but his diary entries record the ups and downs of their long relationship. He described her memorably on first meeting: 'narrow, intelligent face, watching eyes, and a cruel, witty mouth' but 'a body like Donatello's *David*. Those small firm breasts, that modelled neck set with such beauty on her shoulders, that magnificent back'. A year after their affair started, he noted: 'E is sad because she loves me more than I love her. It is sad for me too in another way'. He had numerous other affairs but eventually came to depend on her as much, or more, than she on him. After her death on the 22nd of February 1973 he wrote:

Charles Ritchie

I need to know again from her that I was her life. I would give anything I have to talk to her again, just for an hour. If she ever thought that she loved me more than I did her, she is revenged.

He lived another 22 years, dying in 1995.

[*Love's Civil War: Elizabeth Bowen and Charles Ritchie, Letters and Diaries 1941–1973, edited by Victoria Glendinning with Judith Robertson, Simon & Schuster (2009).*]

J. G. Farrell and Sarah Bond

J. G. Farrell, © Snowdon,
Vogue/Camera Press

Struggling writer J.G. Farrell (33) is trying to make his latest girlfriend, Sarah Bond (24), laugh. He's in a seedy Notting Hill hotel just back from a two-year *sojourn* in New York, where in the final months of his stay he met Sarah. He's breaking his own rules by sending her work-in-progress, but then he knows it's good – it's his masterpiece, *Troubles* – and she did inspire the character named for her, the cruel and fascinating Sarah Devlin. The real Sarah was feisty, independent and malicious, but probably not as malicious as her fictional counterpart. The handsome, depressive Farrell had many girlfriends, none of them long-standing, and he liked Sarah because he believed her 'equally impermeable to romance'. Unwilling to commit, he instead entertained his women with frequent, funny letters. To one he wrote, 'When you do come back, my phone number is 684.7963. I expect you to go straight to Soho and have it tattooed indelibly on your left breast', and to another, 'By the way the only picture I have is the one you don't like. I want one of you preferably with no clothes on.' It's the humour in his letters – even more than the capitals and exclamation marks – that makes them so contemporary. Where 19th- and early-20th-century lovers tend to be in deadly earnest, modern lovers like to make each other laugh – perhaps as a defence mechanism.

STANLEY HOUSE HOTEL
13/14 STANLEY CRESCENT
LONDON W.11
12 July 1968

Sarah dear:

I realise it was my idea to stop writing, you don't have to keep telling me. Blimey – I can't help it if it didn't work, can I? Besides, that was before I'd decided I might come over when I finish my book (though I probably won't).

I had to reach hurriedly for my dark glasses when your letter arrived: though I rather liked the shocking pink, the landlady's dog's hair stood on end when he saw me reading it and he began barking at it, then fled to take refuge under the bed, refusing to come out for half an hour. In the end we had to lure him out with a packet of prime Wiltshire sausages …

I don't believe a word about your 'vast, green jealous complex' re Carol since I remember distinctly you saying how you were never jealous even when your boy-friends slept with other women since you always knew they liked you best. You see, my memory for this sort of thing is prodigious. I wish I could also remember things that would help me make money.

I'm very encouraged that you liked so much of my book [*Troubles*]. It's awfully sloppy and scrappy and inconsistent and inconclusive at the moment. It'll take me years to homogenise it. I've written a bit more but I can't possibly send it for a number of reasons which are too boring to go into. As for the reviews of my first book you can take my word that those idiots don't know what they're talking about. It's as dreary as anything and I don't intend to send it to you …

I was in the public library the other day flicking through a dry and weighty volume of Victorian social history when I came on a love-letter addressed to 'Tony'. Naturally, I read it greedily. Actually, it was only half written … the unnamed girl was begging forgiveness for some unspecified unfaithfulness which had merely been 'experimental' but that ever since 'the first time on the camp bed' (!!!) she had really known that he was the only one. This is the only amusing thing that's happened to me. You are wanted etc.

Love to you,
Jim

P.S. My latest system to fortify myself against the acute attacks of Sarahlessness is to remind myself of how you bit my finger during the 93rd Street Gin and Bathing Festival entirely without provocation.

He was interested enough in Sarah to fly out the following year to New York. But referring to characters in *Troubles*, he had written presciently to her, 'I'm sure that if/when we see each other again we'll both have the feeling the Major has on p.18 when he sees Angela again. One tends to stylize people in one's imagination and the reality comes as a shock ...' and so it proved for him and Sarah. Farrell never married, but then marriage implies settling down and he was peripatetic until *The Siege of Krishnapur* won the Booker, earning him enough money to buy a farmhouse on Sheep's Head Peninsula, Cork, in 1979. He lived there happily for five months until he was swept away to sea while fishing on the 12th of August 1979. His body was found a month later.

[J.G. Farrell, In His Own Image, Selected Letters and Diaries, *edited Lavinia Greacen 2009.]*

Hugh Leonard and Paule Leonard

Hugh Leonard, © Gerray Sweeny, CORBIS (detail)

Septuagenarian playwright Hugh Leonard (Jack Keyes Byrne) is writing to his wife of 45 years, Paule, two weeks after her sudden death on the 13th of April 2000. It is a public letter, published in his weekly *Sunday Independent* column. For fourteen weeks these letters to Paule – 'a record of my coping or failing to cope with the early days of bereavement' – moved his readers. Leonard was so famously caustic that his column was called 'The Curmudgeon'; he and Paule enjoyed a loving but 'prickly' marriage and in his public letters, he was anxious to give a real, not romanticised picture of their life. Paule emerges as loyal, tart and humorous, and gives as good as she gets. Leonard taps into a long tradition of posthumous love; these letters recall Thomas Hardy's poems to his dead wife. This is the only public letter in the book, and it shows. The anecdotes come perfectly timed, the *mot* is always *juste*. Ever the professional, Leonard never forgets his audience. This makes it a more polished read than other letters; inevitably a certain urgency and rawness is lost.

[26 April 2000]
Wednesday

Dear Paule,

Last evening I scalded both my hands because I had forgotten to switch off the hot water. Then in the early hours, I woke up in a dripping sweat; in fact, even the mogs were perspiring, and all because I had omitted to turn off the central heating. This morning, I opened a cupboard to find a plate, and the door fell off.

There is something irresistibly funny about a clumsy male blundering about in what is traditionally a female domain. His wife is either in hospital or away visiting a relative, and he spends his time walking backwards so that he can clean his spoor as he goes. And while I have an almost non-existent sense of smell, yours more than made up for it.

I always half-dreaded your return from, say, visiting cousins in Liege. On the day before your homecoming, I would work myself daft opening windows, vacuuming and scrubbing the sink, but it was vain. You had only to walk in the door after a week's absence, and you were reeling and emitting near-operative cries of 'Faugh!' and 'Phew!' followed by a few fervent 'Yecchs!' which I think you had rehearsed on the plane. And I would slink up to my workroom, muttering 'I hate her!' under my breath.

Well, you aren't ever going to walk in the door again, and in the meantime the cards and messages are still coming. So far there are, at a guess, going on for three hundred of them, more than I can ever hope to reply to personally. All words of counsel are uselsess; the most comforting of them advise me to give thanks that you were spared what I am now going through. Well, that at least makes sense. A tough guy, in an email, tells me, like Duke Wayne admonishing a tenderfoot, 'Get back in the saddle.' Gobshite.

I recall that seven years ago when I underwent a triple cardiac by-pass, I asked a friend to have some flowers delivered to you on my behalf on the morning of the operation. That was not as sadistic as it may seem, for I wanted you to have a just-in-case message which was enclosed with the bouquet. A couple years later, I found the letter, apparently grease-stained, in the kitchen at home.

Rather aggrieved, I asked you either to tear it up or put it away, out of sight of prying eyes. I don't know what you did with it, and I pray that I shall never come across it, for only later did it dawn on me that what I took to be spots of grease were actually tear-stains.

Many of the letters of comfort tell me that one day we, you and I that is, will meet again. That would be nice if it were true, but an irreverent thought occurs to me. Supposing a man or a woman has more than one spouse, how are matters ordered in the hereafter? Does the Almighty put them on a kind of a rota? – Mary on Monday, Wednesday and Friday, and Madge on Tuesday, Thursday, and Saturday, with Sundays to be spent restringing one's harp.

There was a time when I used to refer to you waggishly as 'my present wife'. You took it in good part, even when the joke wore thin; then you learned that a certain lady – in Waterford I think – was declaring as an irrefutable fact that you were my Mate No. 3. So I abandoned the silliness, but the tag endures.

This evening, my dear friend Pat Donlon gave me a precious hour of comfort as well as a splendid dinner, and I told her a story you related to me during our courting days. You warned me that you would deny it, which you certainly did!, if I told another soul. Well, you can't deny it now.

Both your father and uncle Edouard were in the Belgian diplomatic service, and during the Second World War they were both stationed at the embassy in Moscow. When the Germans advanced to within 30 miles of the city, you, with your mother and aunt were sent eastwards by the trans-Siberian railway to Vladivostok and by ship from there to Los Angeles. There you lived out the war and learned English.

(You were born left-handed, but your father would have none of such nonsense and trained you to favour your right hand like 'normal' folk. It was in consequence of this, or so a psychologist once told me, that your brain had a crossover pattern, so that you concocted Spoonerisms. Once, while watching a film about the RAF, you asked me: 'Are those the men who dammed the busts?' And while cruising the Vilaine River in Brittany, you consulted a map and told me that we were 20 miles from Redon, 'as the fly crows'.)

By 1944, the German threat had receded, and your father and uncle were transferred from Moscow to the embassy at Bombay. Meanwhile, an MGM talent scout visited your school and auditioned several girls for a starring role in a film soon to be made. The choice narrowed down to either you or a certain teenage actress a year younger than you, who was already under contract to the studio. A screen test was ordered, and your mother cabled your father in India for his permission.

He refused, replying that he had no wish to see his only child become a spoiled film star brat. You had no acting ambitions and were not in the least perturbed, so the role went by default to the other girl. The film, as it happened, was *National Velvet*.

Another story, one which you told eagerly is that a year or so later, when you went to rejoin your father in India, you travelled by sea via Australia. There, a dockers's strike caused you and your mother and aunt to miss an onward connection from Sydney to Bombay. The vessel you should have taken set sail on the thirteenth of the month and disappeared with all on board in a typhoon in the Indian Ocean. Ever since then, you staunchly regarded thirteen as your lucky number.

(Paule died suddenly on the 13th of April 2000.)

Hugh Leonard, © Gerray Sweeny, CORBIS

[…]
Friday

I sold your car today, didn't haggle, just wanted it gone. That nice man who bought it was virtually my only human contact, apart from people stopping me in the street. What a miserable creature a spoiled husband is! When he is at last alone, he does not know how to look after himself, and if he does know, he doesn't care to. The scales are shifting, though: I am beginning to feel as sorry for myself as for you.

[…]

Sunday […] Later, watching *The Last of the Summer Wine,* I reflected that the writer was making an endless feast of Compos death. The revelation that on Thursdays he secretly visited a gorgeously leggy blonde (Liz Fraser) was pushing it a bit, even if he and she had ferrets in common. You, though, would have laughed a lot and wept a little, and I found myself wanting to tape it for you. No more sharing, aye, there's the rub.

Afterwards I went to La Strada for dinner and tried to reread Maugham's great story, 'The Outstation'. The staff, as always, are kindness itself, but the shrieking of the infants was merciless. I was in sympathy with Anthony Hope, he of the *Prisoner of Zenda,* who on the first night of *Peter Pan* was heard to intone: 'Oh, for an hour of Herod!'

As of midnight, April is over, and thank God for that.

Love,

Jack

A year after Paule's death, Leonard met an American divorcée, Kathy Hayes, on a cruise. He wooed her through emails, as many as ten a day, and they married in June 2007. After eighteen months living with him in Dalkey, she returned for good to America. He died a few weeks later on 12 February 2009; Kathy did not attend his funeral.

Biographies

Allgood, Molly (1887–1952)
Born in Dublin, a daughter of shopkeepers, she was sent to an orphanage after the death of her father but ran away. In 1905 she followed her sister, Sara Allgood, into acting and took the stage name of Máire O'Neill. She was celebrated for her interpretations of J.M. Synge's plays, her fiancé. After his death, she continued her acting career, appearing in many Sean O'Casey plays and in Hitchcock's 1930 film, *Juno and the Paycock*. She was married, widowed, re-married and divorced. She called her daughter Pegeen after her most famous role in *Playboy of the Western World*. (See Synge, John Millington)

Appleby, Eric (d. 1916)
An engineering student from Liverpool, Eric Appleby enlisted in the Royal Field Artillery in 1914 and was posted to Athlone for training. His courtship of Phyllis began when he met her at a dance in Athlone and lasted till his death in the trenches of the Somme in October 1916. (See Kelly, Phyllis)

Barnacle, Nora (1884–1951)
Born and raised in Galway, Nora Barnacle moved to Dublin in early 1904 and worked as a chambermaid in Finn's Hotel on Leinster Street. She met James Joyce that summer and emigrated with him to Italy in October. They lived at numerous addresses in Trieste, Zurich and Paris and had two children, although they didn't marry until 1931 in London. After Joyce's death in 1941, Nora stayed in Zurich, dying of renal failure in 1951. (See Joyce, James)

Berlioz, Hector (1803–1869)
Born near Grenoble in France, Hector Berlioz went to Paris to study medicine in 1821 but, to his parents' disapproval,

soon abandoned medicine for music. An influential Romantic composer and remarkable interpreter of Shakespeare, he made great advancements in the area of orchestration and was also a notable music critic. He was histrionic and fell rapidly in love. After the death of his first wife, Harriet Smithson, in 1854, he remarried immediately; widowed again eight years later, he attempted unsuccessfully to re-marry for a third time. (See Smithson, Harriet)

Boland, Harry (1887–1922)

Born in Dublin, the son of a Fenian and GAA official, Harry emulated his father by joining the IRB and the GAA, and was a founder member of the Irish Volunteers. He fought in the GPO in 1916. In 1922 he took the anti-treaty side against his former best friend, Michael Collins. He was shot by Free State soldiers at the Grand Hotel in Skerries and died on the 1st of August 1922 in St Vincent's Hospital. His funeral in Glasnevin was massively attended. (See Kiernan, Kitty)

Bond, Sarah (b. 1944)

English girl who met J.G. Farrell in New York and proved the inspiration for the character of Sarah Devlin in *Troubles*. (See J.G. Farrell)

Harry Boland

Bowen, Elizabeth (1899–1973)

Born in Dublin to an Anglo-Irish family, she spent childhood summers in the family home, Bowen's Court, Co. Cork. She married an English civil servant, lived in London, had numerous affairs and was critically acclaimed for her novels, including *The Last September* and *Death of the Heart*. In the 1940s and '50s she moved between London and Bowen's Court, but in 1959 she was forced to sell the Cork family home. (See Ritchie, Charles)

Bright, Reginald Golding (1875–1941)

Born at Lewisham, Kent, he was a drama critic and literary and theatrical agent for Bernard Shaw and Somerset Maugham. His brother, Addison, was agent for J.M. Barrie and committed suicide after he was found to have misappropriated funds. Reginald predeceased his much older wife, George Egerton, and left her almost penniless. (See Egerton, George)

Campbell, Mrs Patrick (1865–1940)

Born Beatrice Stella Tanner in London, she made her professional debut in Liverpool in 1888 and in New York in 1900. She appeared, at age 49, in the 1914 West End production of Shaw's *Pygmalion* as the flower girl, Eliza Doolittle, but refused, at age 73, to play Professor Higgins' mother in the 1938 film of the play. She was married twice and had two children. (See Shaw, George Bernard)

Ceannt, Áine (1880–1954)

Born Frances Mary O'Brennan in Dublin, the daughter of an auctioneer and former Fenian, she joined the Gaelic League in 1901 and gaelicised her name. She had been married eleven years to Eamonn Ceannt when he was executed as a 1916 leader. She became a founding member of the Irish White Cross, held a senior role in Cumann na mBan, was a district judge in the Sinn Féin courts and brought up their only son, Rónán. She died in Dundrum, Dublin. (See Ceannt, Eamonn)

Ceannt, Eamonn (1881–1916)
Born Edward Kent in Glenamaddy, Galway, son of an RIC constable, Eamonn Ceannt worked as a clerk for Dublin Corporation. He joined the Gaelic League in 1899, Sinn Féin in 1907 and the Irish Volunteers in 1913. As one of the seven signatories of the Proclamation of the Republic and commander of a battalion at the South Dublin Union, he was executed on the 8th of May 1916. (See Ceannt, Áine)

Collins, Michael (1890–1922)
Born in west Cork, Michael Collins left school at 15 and worked as a clerk in London. He joined the Irish Volunteers in 1914 and played a backroom role in the GPO in 1916. Elected to the Sinn Féin executive in 1917, he was returned unopposed to the Dáil for Cork South. The central military organiser of the war of independence, 1919–1921, he was on the negotiating team for the Anglo-Irish Treaty of December 1921. Chairman of the first provisional government and minister for finance, he was shot in an ambush at Béal na mBláth, Co. Cork, in August 1922. (See Kiernan, Kitty)

Congreve, William (1670–1729)
Born in Yorkshire, William Congreve was reared and educated in Ireland and entered Trinity College Dublin in 1686. He afterwards lived mostly in London. Like his friend, Jonathan Swift, he was a strong Tory. A notable Restoration playwright, his most famous works include *Love for Love* (1695) and *The Way of the World* (1700). He died in 1729 in London, possibly from injuries following a carriage accident. (See Hunt, Arabella)

Crawford, Alexander (b. 1855)
Born in Belfast, he emigrated to Australia about 1881 and worked as a sheep farmer. He married his cousin, Elizabeth Matthews, and on her death married her sister, Martha. Widowed again, he

married a much younger woman. He had four children. (See Matthews, Elizabeth)

Cunard, Lady Maud (1872–1948)

Born Maud Alice Burke in San Francisco to an Irish-American family, she was educated in New York. After being jilted by a Polish prince, she married the much older Sir Bache Cunard of the shipping line and moved with him to England. A notable society hostess, in later years, after the death of her husband, she was known as 'Emerald'. Her daughter was the celebrated and radical writer and muse Nancy Cunard. (See Moore, George)

Curran, Sarah (1782–1808)

Born in Cork, daughter of the famous Irish lawyer John Philpot Curran, she was raised in Dublin in an unhappy home. She was introduced to the radical Robert Emmet by her brother. Their relationship remained a secret and when it was revealed after Emmet's arrest, her father threw her out of the house. After Emmet's execution, she married, had a child that lived but died herself shortly afterwards of tuberculosis. (See Emmet, Robert)

Sarah Curran (detail)

206

Davis, Thomas (1814–1845)

Born in Mallow, Co. Cork, the son of a military surgeon, Thomas Davis achieved fame early as journalist with *The Nation* and as a poet and balladeer. The most famous of his songs 'The West's asleep' and 'A nation once again' are still sung. Originally a fervent O'Connellite, he disagreed with the Liberator over the ethics of physical force and other matters. This flared into open argument in 1845, a few months before Davis' death from scarlet fever. Thousands followed his funeral cortege to Mount Jerome cemetery. (See Hutton, Annie)

Douglas, Lord Alfred (1870–1945)

Born in Worcestershire, the third son of the 9th Marquess of Queensberry, Lord Alfred Douglas, or 'Bosie', so called for a childhood nickname, was educated at Winchester College and Oxford. He first met Oscar Wilde in 1891 and they began a passionate affair which survived Wilde's imprisonment. Following Wilde's death in 1900, Douglas married Olive Eleanor Custance, an heiress and poet, and spent the rest of his life alternating between repudiating Wilde, writing about their relationship and suing Wildean scholars for defamation. (See Wilde, Oscar)

Draper, Eliza (1744–1778)

Born in India as Eliza Sclater, she was orphaned young and educated in England. At the age of 14 she married an older man, Daniel Draper, in Bombay and had three children. While in England in 1767, settling her children into boarding school, Eliza met the writer, Laurence Sterne, who became infatuated with her and ensured her immortality. She died in England, aged 34. (See Sterne, Laurence)

Duncannon, Lady Harriet (1761–1821)

Born Lady Henrietta Frances Spencer in Wimbledon, she was sister of the notorious

Georgiana, Duchess of Devonshire, and an ancestor of Diana, Princess of Wales. She married Viscount Duncannon (later Lord Bessborough) and had numerous affairs, including an embarrassingly public one with the playwright, Richard Brinsley Sheridan. (See Sheridan, Richard Brinsley)

Emmet, Robert (1778–1803)

Born in Dublin, son of the state physician and brother of the United Irishman Thomas Addis Emmet, Robert was expelled from Trinity College in 1798 for his links with the United Irishmen. He planned and led the doomed 1803 rebellion but is most famous for his remarkable speech from the dock. Convicted of high treason, he was executed in 1803 on Dublin's Thomas Street. (See Curran, Sarah)

Egerton, George (1859–1945)

Born Mary Chavelita Dunne in Melbourne, Australia, daughter of an Irish army officer, she was educated in Ireland and trained as a nurse in London. As George Egerton, she was a noted feminist writer before the word 'feminist' became well known. Her short story collection *Keynotes* caused a sensation on both sides of the Atlantic. Married three times, she was an advocate of women's sexual rights far ahead of her time. (See Bright, Reginald Golding)

Farrell, James Gordon (1935–1979)

Born in Liverpool, he moved with his family to Dalkey, Dublin, in 1947. After Oxford he concentrated on writing. After two trial novels, he achieved success quickly: *Troubles* (1970) won him the Faber memorial prize and *The Siege of Krishnapur* won the Booker. In 1979 he moved to Sheep's Head Peninsula, where he died while angling off the rocks below his house. He was posthumously awarded the Lost Man Booker Prize in 2010 for *Troubles*. (See Bond, Sarah)

Ford, John (1894–1973)

Born John Feeney in Maine, son of a Galway father and Aran Islands mother, he was among America's most ground-breaking film directors. In a career spanning almost fifty years, he directed over 140 films and won four Academy Awards for Best Directing. His best-remembered films include *The Informer, The Grapes of Wrath, How Green Was My Valley* and *The Quiet Man*. (See O'Hara, Maureen)

Gifford, Grace (1888–1955)

Born Grace Evelyn Gifford in Dublin to a Catholic father and protestant mother, her drawing talent as a child garnered the praise of John B. Yeats. She attended the Metropolitan School of Art in Dublin and the Slade School in London. Aged 28, she married Joseph Mary Plunkett in Kilmainham Gaol in 1916 and became, like her sister Muriel, a 1916 widow. She never remarried, remained a Republican and earned a precarious living as an artist and cartoonist. (See Plunkett, Joseph Mary)

Gifford, Muriel (1884–1917)

Older sister of Grace Gifford, Muriel trained as a nurse, was politically active like her sisters and married the revolutionary Thomas MacDonagh in January 1912. They had two children. Barely a year after MacDonagh's execution in 1916, she died of heart failure while swimming in Skerries, Co. Dublin. (See MacDonagh, Thomas)

Gonne, Iseult (1894–1954)

Born in France, the illegitimate daughter of Maud Gonne and her married lover Lucien Millevoye, Iseult was passed off in society as Maud's niece. A highly intelligent and beautiful young woman, she rejected Yeats' proposal of marriage and in 1920 married the 17-year-old Francis Stuart. They had two surviving children but their marriage was difficult and ended in separation. (See Pound, Ezra)

Gonne, Maud (1866–1953)

Born in Surrey the daughter of an army officer, she was educated in Ireland and London and by the age of 20 was a confirmed Irish nationalist. Independently wealthy, she devoted herself to the cause of Irish independence. Her charisma and beauty won her numerous admirers, most notably including W.B. Yeats. She had two children (one deceased) with her French lover, Lucien Millevoye, and one son, Sean MacBride, with her husband, Major John MacBride, whom she soon divorced. She refused numerous offers of marriage from Yeats but they remained friends for life. (See Yeats, W.B.)

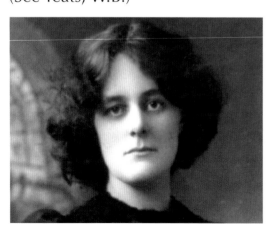

Maud Gonne

Greene, Sheila May (*fl.*1940)

Born Sheila May, she was a political activist and an actress associated with the Gate Theatre. She married and divorced the noted Celtic scholar, David Greene. Her only child, Vicky, was the result of a liaison with the physicist Erwin Schrödinger. (See Schrödinger, Erwin)

Holland, Constance (1859–1898)

Born Constance Lloyd, daughter of a barrister, she married Wilde in 1884 and had two sons. After Wilde's imprisonment, she changed the family name to Holland to spare her children scandal. She didn't divorce Wilde but refused him financial support when he returned to Lord Alfred Douglas after his imprisonment. She died following spinal surgery and is buried in Genoa in Italy. Wilde died two years later, leaving their sons orphans. (See Wilde, Oscar)

Hunt, Arabella (1662–1705)

A celebrated beauty, lutenist and

singer, she gave lessons in the royal household. The composers Henry Purcell and John Blow wrote difficult music for her. (See Congreve, William)

Hutton, Annie (1825–1853)

Daughter of a Dublin Protestant merchant, Annie Hutton fell in love with Thomas Davis in 1843, when she was 18 and he 29, but had to wait two years to become engaged since her parents initially opposed the match. Weakened by Davis' sudden death, and in fragile health herself, Annie died in the summer of 1853. (See Davis, Thomas)

Johnson, Esther (1681–1728)

Born in Surrey, Esther (or Hester) Johnson was the daughter of the housekeeper of Sir William Temple (and rumoured to be Temple's illegitimate daughter). When Jonathan Swift was appointed Temple's secretary, he acted as her tutor and grew devoted to her, nicknaming her 'Stella'. In 1699 he persuaded her

and a companion to move near to him in Dublin. The exact nature of their relationship remains a mystery. (See Swift, Jonathan)

Joyce, James (1882–1941)

Born in Dublin and educated by the Jesuits in Clongowes, Belvedere and University College Dublin, James Joyce left Dublin for good in 1904, when he eloped with the Galway chambermaid, Nora Barnacle. They lived a nomadic lifestyle with their two children in Trieste, Zurich and Paris. With the publication of *Ulysses* in 1922 he became perhaps the most famous and least-read author in the world. He died at the age of 59 in Zurich. (See Barnacle, Nora)

Kavanagh, Patrick (1904–1967)

Born in Monaghan, son of a farmer, he worked for decades as a full-time farmer and part-time poet until he moved to London in 1937 and two years later settled in Dublin. Most famous for his long poem 'The

Great Hunger' and for 'Raglan Road', which he wrote for Luke Kelly to sing. He died in Dublin in 1967, a few days after the opening performance of the stage adaptation of his novel *Tarry Flynn*. (See Moriarty,Hilda)

Kearney, Eva *(fl.* 1914)

Born Eva Flanagan, she married Peadar Kearney in 1914 and had two sons, Pearse and Con. (See Kearney, Peadar)

Kearney, Peadar (1883–1942)

Born in Dublin, son of a grocer, he joined the Gaelic League in 1901 and the IRB soon after. His talents were various: he was stage manager for the Abbey Theatre and a playwright, but it's as a songwriter that he's most remembered (he wrote the national anthem). He quit an Abbey tour in England to take part in the Rising and fought in Jacob's factory. After fighting in the War of Independence he took the pro-Treaty side. His sister was Kathleen Kearney, mother of Brendan Behan. (See Kearney, Eva)

Kelly, Phyllis (born c. 1894)

Phyllis Kelly was the daughter of an Athlone solicitor. In 1915 she became engaged to an English soldier, Eric Appleby, when he was sent to Athlone for military training. He died in the trenches in 1916. (See Appleby, Eric)

Kiernan, Kitty (1893–1945)

Born in Longford, daughter of a hotelier, she was orphaned at the age of 15. She and her siblings ran the family hotel, bar, bakery and shop. She met both Harry Boland and Michael Collins in 1917/18. Boland was first to show interest in her but she preferred Collins. Their engagement was announced in the Dáil in January 1922 but Collins was killed eight months later, three weeks after Boland. She married an army officer, Felix Cronin, had two sons and died of kidney disease in 1945. (See Collins, Michael)

Leonard, Hugh (1926–2009)

Born John Joseph Byrne in Dublin, he was adopted and changed his name to John Keyes Byrne, taking Hugh Leonard as a pen name. He worked as a civil servant for 14 years before becoming a full-time writer. He had great success as a TV scriptwriter, playwright and columnist, and his play *Da* won him a Tony award and was made into a film in 1988. His 'curmudgeonly' weekly columns in the *Sunday Independent* gained him a national readership. (See Leonard, Paule)

Leonard, Paule (d. 2000)

Born in Belgium, she married Jack Byrne ('Hugh Leonard') in 1955 and moved with him to London and then to Dalkey. They had one daughter, Danielle. (See Leonard, Hugh)

Lockett, Alice (1858–1942)

Born in England into a middle-class family, Alice Lockett met George Bernard Shaw in 1883 when she was a nursing student and he was recovering from scarlet fever. She was the first recipient of his remarkable love letters. Afterwards they remained friends; she was almost as long-lived as him. (See Shaw, George Bernard)

mac Crimthainn, Áed (died c. 1201)

Born into a Co. Laois family, he was Abbot of Tír-Dá-Glas monastery and is the only known scribe of the *Book of Leinster*. (See Ua Gormain, Finn)

MacDonagh, Thomas (1878–1916)

Born in Tipperary, son of a national school teacher, Thomas MacDonagh originally trained for the priesthood, but left to become a teacher and writer. He joined the Gaelic League in 1901 and began teaching in Pearse's Irish-language school, St Enda's, in 1908, before becoming a lecturer in UCD. He joined the Irish Volunteers and, as one of the signatories of the Proclamation of the Irish Republic, was executed by firing squad on the 3rd of May 1916. (See Gifford, Muriel)

McCracken, Mary Ann (1770–1866)

Born in Belfast, she was sister of the United Irishman, Henry Joy McCracken, who was executed for his part in the 1798 rebellion. In her long, useful life, she championed the rights of women, campaigned for the abolition of the slave trade and helped famine victims and the destitute. (See Russell, Thomas)

Martin, Violet ('Martin Ross') (1862–1915)

Born in Ross House, Co. Galway, to an Anglo-Irish landowner, her twin interests from an early age were horse riding and literature. Her partnership and literary collaboration with her distant cousin Edith Somerville began soon after they met in 1886. She suffered a serious horse-riding accident in 1898 and was in pain for the rest of her life. She died in Cork of a brain tumour. (See Somerville, Edith)

Mathews, Elizabeth (d. 1891)

She emigrated from Ireland as a child and settled with her family in Victoria, Australia. She married her distant cousin Alexander Crawford in 1885 but died six years later. (See Crawford, Alexander)

Moore, George (1852–1933)

Born to Catholic landed gentry in Ballyglass, Mayo, Moore studied art in Paris and London before concentrating on writing. Influenced by Zola, his novels are naturalistic, take on daring themes and were highly rated by Joyce. A key figure in the Irish Literary Revival, he caused offense with the portrayal of friends in his autobiography, published in 1911. He died in 1933 in London. (See Cunard, Lady Maud)

Moriarty, Hilda (1923–1991)

Born in Dingle, Co. Kerry, she came to Dublin to study medicine. A muse for Patrick

Kavanagh and the inspiration for 'Raglan Road', she married Donogh O'Malley, an engineering student from Limerick, who was later Fianna Fáil Minister for Education. They had two children. After her husband's sudden death, she unsuccessfully sought the party nomination for his seat and then stood as an independent candidate in the by-election, but was defeated by Donogh's nephew, Desmond O'Malley. (See Kavanagh, Patrick)

Murdoch, Iris (1919–1999)
Born in Dublin, daughter of a civil servant, she gained a First in Mods and Greats from Oxford and published her first novel, *Under the Net,* in 1954. She was famous as a prolific author of novels on philosophical themes before her diagnosis with Alzheimer's in 1997. She was nursed lovingly through her illness by her husband, John Bayley. (See Thompson, Frank)

O' Connell, Daniel (1775–1848)
Born in Caherciveen, Co. Kerry, to Catholic landed gentry, Daniel O'Connell was educated in France and London and had a remarkable career as a barrister before embarking on his even more remarkable career as a politician. His crowning success was Catholic Emancipation in 1829. He had less success with his campaign to repeal the Union, but proved his popularity and the popularity of his politics with the numbers he mustered for the monster meetings of the early 1840s. Bestowed the title of 'Liberator' by the people of Ireland, he died in Genoa. (See O'Connell, Mary)

O' Connell, Mary (1778–1836)
Born in Tralee, she was a distant cousin of Daniel O'Connell, whom she married in 1802, secretly as his family initially opposed the match. Despite his financial imprudence and rumours of his philandering, the marriage was loving and resulted in seven children. (See O'Connell, Daniel)

O'Donnell, Annie (1880–1959)
Born in Spiddal, Co. Galway, she was the second-youngest of

seven children. She emigrated to America at the age of 18 to join her elder sisters and worked as a nursery maid in Pittsburgh. She married Kilkenny-born James Phelan in 1904 and had eight children, six surviving to adulthood. (See Phelan, James)

O'Flaherty, Liam (1896–1984)

Born in the Aran Islands, one of 14 children of a smallholding farmer, he was intended for the priesthood but left to study in UCD. He joined the Volunteers but, tired of waiting for the Rising, enlisted in the Irish Guards, fought in France and was seriously wounded. A communist, his most famous novel was *The Informer*. His first marriage was unhappy, but his second was successful. (See Tailer, Kitty)

O' Hara, Maureen (b. 1920)

Born Maureen FitzSimons in Dublin, daughter of a merchant and a former opera singer, her potential was spotted by Charles Laughton in a London screen test and she went on to a Hollywood career. Her striking colouring – red hair and green eyes – was showcased by the move from black-and-white to technicolour. She made five features with director John Ford. She married three times and now lives mainly in Glengariff, Co. Cork. (See Ford, John)

O'Shea, Katherine (1846–1921)

Born Katherine Wood in Braintree, Essex, daughter of a baronet clergyman, she married Captain William O'Shea in 1867. In 1880 she met Parnell and they began a passionate affair, which led to three children (two surviving infancy) and his political downfall. They married in June 1891; he died less than four months later. She lived on until the age of 75. (See Parnell, Charles Stewart)

Ogle, Esther Jane (1773–1817)

Youngest of the five daughters of the dean of Winchester and toasted 'the irresistible Ogle' by the Kit-Kat Club, she married

Richard Brinsley Sheridan in 1795 and was mother of his son, Charles. She survived her husband by only 14 months. (See Sheridan, Richard Brinsley)

Parnell, Charles Stewart (1846–1891)

Born in Wicklow to an Anglo-Irish landowner, he was elected for Meath in 1875 and by 1880 was president of the Land League and chairman of the Irish party in Westminster. He triumphantly survived imprisonment, a defeated home rule bill and an attempt by the *Times* newspaper to link him to the Phoenix Park murders, but was ultimately brought down by his private life when Captain William O'Shea sued for divorce in December 1889, citing him as correspondent. His party abandoned him and he died soon after. (See O'Shea, Katherine 'Kitty')

Phelan, James (1876–1961)

Born in Kilkenny, he worked as a farmer before emigrating to America in 1898 and settling in Indianapolis. He married Annie O'Donnell in 1904, settled in Pittsburgh and had eight children, six surviving. He outlived his wife by two years, dying at the age of 85. (See O'Donnell, Annie)

Plunkett, Joseph Mary (1887–1916)

Born in Dublin, son of a barrister and a papal count from an ancient family, he had a more moneyed, privileged background than any other of the 1916 leaders. A gifted poet, he suffered chronically poor health from childhood – tuberculosis, pleurisy and pneumonia – so was more a military planner than active soldier. He married Grace Gifford in his Kilmainham cell, just hours before his execution. (See Gifford, Grace)

Pound, Ezra (1885–1972)

Born in Idaho, he emigrated to Europe in 1908 and settled in London (1908–1920), Paris

(1921–1924) and Italy (1924–1945). A fine Imagist poet, he is noted for his influence on and generosity towards other writers, including Yeats, Eliot and Joyce. A key figure in the modernist movement, his legacy is tainted by his anti-Semitism during the war. He was charged with treason in the United States, but deemed unfit to stand trial and was incarcerated for 12 years in a mental asylum. (See Gonne, Iseult)

Ritchie, Charles (1906–1995)

Born in Halifax, Nova Scotia, Charles Ritchie was successively Canada's ambassador to West Germany (1954–1958), Permanent Representative to the United Nations (1958–1962), ambassador to the United States (1962–1966), ambassador to the North Atlantic Council (1966–1967) and Canadian High Commissioner to the United Kingdom in London (1967–1971). A regular diarist, he published *The Siren Years: A Canadian Diplomat Abroad (1974)*. (See Bowen, Elizabeth)

Ruddock, Margot (1907–1951)

Actress, poet and singer, with thestage name 'Margot Collis', she married twice and Yeats was briefly infatuated with her. She suffered from depression and was committed permanently to a mental institution in 1937. (See Yeats, W.B.)

Russell, Thomas (1767–1803)

Born near Mallow, Cork, the youngest child of an army lieutenant, he was co-founder of the United Irishmen and a close friend of Wolfe Tone and Henry Joy McCracken. Imprisoned without trial for six years from 1796, he missed the 1798 rebellion but helped plan Robert Emmet's 1803 rising in Dublin and attempted to raise Ulster. He was hanged in Downpatrick Gaol and is the subject of the ballad 'The Man from God Knows Where'. (See McCracken, Mary Ann)

Schrödinger, Erwin (1887–1961)
Born in Vienna, he was a physicist and theoretical biologist and a father of quantum mechanics, who received the Nobel Prize for Physics in 1933 for the 'Schrödinger equation' on wave mechanics. When Hitler invaded Austria in 1938, Schrödinger accepted an invitation from Éamon de Valera to a post at the Institute for Advanced Studies in Dublin. He remained in Ireland for 17 years, eventually returning to Vienna in 1956, where he died of tuberculosis in 1961. (See Greene, Sheila May)

Shaw, George Bernard (1856–1950)
Born in Dublin, son of a civil servant, he left Ireland permanently for London in 1876. His rise was slow but by the 1890s he was probably the most famous theatre critic in London and with *Arms and the Man* (premiered in 1894) he embarked on his enormously successful career as dramatist. A socialist, teetotaller, vegetarian and home-ruler, he won the Nobel Prize for Literature in 1925 and has given the adjective 'Shavian' to the language. He married and adored women, but more for flirtation than sex. (See Lockett, Alice)

Sheehy, Hanna (1877–1946)
Born in Cork, daughter of a nationalist MP, she was educated in Dublin and met her future husband, Francis Skeffington, as a student. He influenced her in her feminism and political radicalism, for which she was jailed. She was until the end of her long life an active campaigner and motivator. After her husband's murder in 1916, she supported herself and her son through her journalism. (See Skeffington, Frank)

Skeffington, Frank (1878–1916)
Born in Co. Cavan, the only child of a school inspector, he was, from the time he attended UCD, famous for his eccentric attire, his brilliance and his radical views on vegetarianism, pacifism and

feminism. A noted journalist and political campaigner, he combined his name with his wife's, Hanna Sheehy, when they married in 1903. His execution without trial in Easter Week, when he had taken no part in the fighting, helped turn the public mood against the government. (See Sheehy, Hanna)

Sheridan, Richard Brinsley (1751–1816)

Born in Dublin, son of the manager of the Smock Alley Theatre, he married, very young, the famous singer Eliza Linley and wrote his first play, *The Rivals* (1775), to support them. He combined success as a playwright with politics and sat as a Whig for Stafford (1780–1806). Co-owner of the Drury Lane Theatre, he was financially ruined when it burnt down in 1809. (See Duncannon, Lady Harriet; Ogle, Esther Jane)

Smithson, Harriet (1800–1854)

Born in Ennis, daughter of an actor, she made her stage debut in Dublin as a 14-year-old. Her exquisite looks, rather than acting ability, wowed audiences and, fatally for her, attracted the attention of the melodramatic composer, Hector Berlioz. She agreed to marry him, but was made almost immediately unhappy, and after a series of strokes died in Paris. (See Berlioz, Hector)

Somerville, Edith (1858–1949)

Born in Corfu to an Anglo-Irish family, she was raised in the family estate in Castletownshend, Cork. She studied art in London and Paris and from 1887 began collaborating on a famous series of novels with her partner and distant cousin, Violet Martin. After Martin's early death, she retained their joint names 'Somerville and Ross' on the books she produced alone. (See Ross, Martin)

Sterne, Laurence (1713–1768)

Born in Clonmel, son of an English army officer, he was ordained a priest in the Church of England in 1738. A tedious existence as a clergyman was relieved by the publication and immediate fame of *The Life and Opinions of Tristram Shandy,* appearing in nine volumes from 1759–1767. The last few years of his life were as excitable and exciting as his temperament demanded. (See Draper, Eliza)

Swift, Jonathan (1667–1745)

Born in Dublin to English parents, he was educated at Trinity College Dublin and Oxford. Ordained as an Anglican priest in 1695, his fame as a satirist and author of *Gulliver's Travels* was enormous, though he mostly published anonymously or pseudonymously. His happiest period was spent in London as a Tory propagandist from 1707-1714; thereafter he was confined to Dublin as Dean of St Patrick's. He never married, but his relations with women have fascinated readers for three centuries. (See Waring, Jane; Johnson, Esther; Vanhomrigh, Esther)

Synge, John Millington (1871–1909)

Born in Dublin to an Anglo-Irish family, Synge was frail from infancy and was largely educated at home. The Aran Islands and west of Ireland provided the inspiration for his work, including the seminal *Playboy of the Western World* and *Riders to the Sea.* He died young of Hodgkin's lymphoma. (See Allgood, Molly)

Tailer, Kitty (d. 1990)

Born Kitty Harding, she was an American divorcée with two sons when she met Liam O'Flaherty in Santa Barbara, California. They married and lived in Connecticut before settling in Dublin in 1952. (See O'Flaherty, Liam)

Thompson, Frank (1920–1944)

Born in 1920 in West Bengal, William Frank Thompson met Iris Murdoch while studying at Oxford. He volunteered to join the British Army during World War II and, since he spoke nine languages, became liaison officer between the army and the Bulgarian resistance, with whose aims he was sympathetic. He was captured and executed in 1944. (See Murdoch, Iris)

Tone, Matilda (1869–1849)

Born Matilda Witherington in Dublin to a family of drapers, she eloped with the revolutionary, Theobald Wolfe Tone, one month after her 16th birthday. She shared his political interests and was his companion and confidante. After his death, she moved to America, remarried and published Tone's remarkable writings with her son, William. (See Tone, Theobald Wolfe)

Tone, Theobald Wolfe (1763–1798)

Born in Dublin to a middle-class protestant family, he was called to the bar in 1789 after a chequered student career. Uninterested in law, he turned to pamphleteering and set up the United Irishmen with Thomas Russell in 1791. He campaigned in America and France. The first-planned French expedition to Ireland in December 1796 ended in failure, due to bad weather. The next, in August 1798, was equally doomed and ended in Tone's capture and his suicide. His wonderful memoirs and letters helped his posthumous fame. (See Tone, Matilda, née Witherington)

Ua Gormain, Finn, Bishop of Kildare (d. AD 1160)

From an old north Leinster dynasty, he followed Cistercian monastic observance and was Abbot of Newry, Co. Down. He was elected Bishop of Kildare during the 1150s and died in AD 1160. (See macCrimthainn, Áed)

Vanhomrigh, Esther ('Vanessa') (1688–1723)

Born in Dublin, daughter of a wealthy merchant, she lived briefly in London where she met Jonathan Swift. She followed him to Dublin and remained obsessed with him till the end of her brief life. He wrote the poem

'Cadenus and Vanessa' about the relationship. (See Swift, Jonathan)

Waring, Jane (*fl.* 1700)

Daughter of the Archdeacon of Dromore, she was the only woman to receive a marriage proposal from Jonathan Swift. She vacillated and incensed him and after 1700 they broke off all relations. (See Swift, Jonathan)

Wilde, Oscar (1854–1900)

Born in Dublin into a noted intellectual and eccentric family, he attended Trinity College but left Ireland permanently in 1874. His enormous London success as playwright, essayist, wit and aesthete was shattered by his arrest and imprisonment for homosexuality in 1895, but his imprisonment has since helped turn him into one of the most iconic figures in history. (See Holland, Constance; Douglas, Lord Alfred)

Yeats, W.B. (1865–1939)

Born in Dublin, son of the painter John B. Yeats, he was raised in Sligo, Dublin and London. The foremost Irish poet writing in English and a key figure in modernism and the Irish literary revival, he was co-founder of the Abbey Theatre and ended life as a senator. (See Gonne, Maud; Ruddock, Margot)

Acknowledgements

3 Sterne's Eliza, © Laurence Sterne Trust, used with permission

6 Katherine O'Shea, Library of Congress

7 Michael Collins, courtesy of www.generalmichaelcollins.com

9 Oscar Wilde / Napoleon Sarony, Wikipedia Commons

9 Lord Alfred Bruce Douglas / George Charles Beresford © National Portrait Gallery

10 Esther Vanhomrigh, by Sir John Everett Millais, courtesy of National Museums, Liverpool

13 George Moore, by Edouard Manet. Image © The Metropolitan Museum of Art /Scala Archive

14 Maud Gonne, Library of Congress

15 William Butler Yeats, by George Charles Beresford / © National Portrait Gallery, London

16 Éamonn Ceannt, The Unbroken Tradition, by Nora Connolly O'Brien, Boni & Liveright

19 Maud Gonne, Library of Congress

21 Maud Gonne and W. B. Yeats, by John Nolan, © John Nolan

26 Letter, Wikipedia Commons

26 Map, Wikipedia Commons

28 Sir Frederic William Burton (1816–1900) Hellelil and Hildebrand, the Meeting on the Turret Stairs, 1864, © National Gallery of Ireland

30 Smith, I; after Kneller, G, Sir., Mrs Arabella Hunt (1662–1705)' from volume 1706 (mezzotint) © The Hunterian, University of Glasgow, 2011

30 William Congreve, TPL

31 Anne Bracegirdle, Wikipedia Commons

32 Jonathan Swift, Wikipedia Commons

32 Varina, Unknown

35 Jonathan Swift by Charles Jervas, oil on canvas, c.1718, © National Portrait Gallery, London

37 Gulliver's Travels, Library of Congress

38 Stella, Sir John Everett Millais, Manchester Art Gallery, The Bridgeman Art Library

40 Swift, Library of Congress

41 Swift death mask, Library of Congress

43 Vanessa, by Millais, Courtesy of National Museums Liverpool

45 George Berkeley, Yale University Manuscripts & Archives

46 Laurence Sterne by Sir Joshua Reynolds, © National Portrait Gallery, London

49 Portrait (detail) by Richard Cosway. Private collection. Used with permission of The Laurence Sterne Trust.

50 Sterne's Eliza, © Laurence Sterne Trust, used with permission

51 Sheridan, engraving, TPL

52 Mrs. Richard Brinsley Sheridan, c.1785–87 (oil on canvas) by Gainsborough, Thomas (1727–88), Mellon Coll., Nat. Gallery of Art, Washington DC, USA / The Bridgeman Art Library

55 New Drury Lane Theatre, engraving, TPL

56 Wolfe Tone, TPL

57 James Gillray, Library of Congress

61 Mary O'Connell and her youngest son Daniel by Gubbins, Derrynane House, Caherdaniel. By kind permission of Adrian Corcoran, The Office of Public Works, Killarney. Photograph by Barbara Hodges

61 Daniel O'Connell, Library of Congress

63 Daniel O'Connell by Bernard Mulrenin, © National Portrait Gallery, London.

64 Daniel O'Connell, engraving by W. Hall, TPL

65 Sarah Curran by George Romney, Wikipedia Commons

65 Robert Emmet, TPL

67 Sarah Curran Playing the Harp by William Beechey 1805, Calderdale MBC Museums and Galleries

68 John Philpot Curran by unknown artist, oil on canvas, © National Portrait Gallery, London

70 The execution of Robert Emmet, Library of Congress

71 Mary Ann McCracken, unknown

71 From Richard R. Madden, The United Irishmen, Their Lives and Times 1860

72 The United Irish Patriots of 1798 after unknown artist, © National Portrait Gallery, London

74 Henrietta Smithson, Wikipedia Commons

74 Hector Berlioz, Wikipedia Commons, source Berkshire Fine Arts

75 Franz Liszt, Library of Congress

76 Hector Berlioz, Library of Congress

77 Thomas Davis, The Memoirs of an Irish Patriot, 1840-1846. Kegan Paul, Trench, Trubner & Co. Ltd. 1890, Wikipedia Commons

77 Annie Hutton, from the painting by Sir Frederic Burton: Michael Quigley, Pictorial Record, Centenary of Thomas Davis and Young Ireland (Dublin 1945)

80 Charles Stewart Parnell, Library of Congress

80 Kitty O'Shea, unknown

81 William O'Shea, Wikipedia Commons

82 Parnell addressing The Irish Parliamentary Party, Library of Congress

84 George Bernard Shaw, cigarette card, TPL

85 A playbill for Bernard Shaw's Captain Brassbound's Conversion, Library of Congress

86 George Bernard Shaw, Library of Congress

86 Drawing of Eliza Doolittle from Shaw's play Pygmalion, Library of Congress

87 George Bernard Shaw, Library of Congress

88 George Bernard Shaw, Library of Congress

89 Mrs Campbell, Library of Congress

91 Mrs Campbell, Library of Congress

92 19th-century Belfast, unknown

93 Emigrants readying for departure, Library of Congress

94 1880s Australian sheep station, Library of Congress

95 Ballarat, 1880s, Library of Congress

97 Families disembark at port in Australia, TPL

98 Student at Colarossis Studio, Paris, pencil on paper, Edith Somerville, courtesy of Crawford Art Gallery, Cork

99 The Goose Girl, Edith Somerville, courtesy of Crawford Art Gallery, Cork

100 A Holy Place of Druids, oil on canvas, Edith Somerville, courtesy of Crawford Art Gallery, Cork

101 Interior of Colarossis Studio, Paris, pencil on paper, Edith Somerville, courtesy of Crawford Art Gallery, Cork

103 Grave Stone of Somerville, 1998, John Minihan, black and white photograph, courtesy of Crawford Art Gallery, Cork

104 Oscar Wilde, Napoleon Sarony, Wikipedia Commons

104 Constance Holland, Wikipedia Commons

105 Constance to Arthur Humphreys, compilation of Wildean wit, Oscariana

106 Oscar Wilde, Napoleon Sarony, Wikipedia Commons

106 Lord Alfred Douglas, George Charles Beresford, © National Portrait Gallery, London

107 Police News, Wikipedia Commons

109 Oscar Wilde; Lord Alfred Bruce Douglas by Gillman & Cosilver, gelatin print, © National Portrait Gallery, London

110 Mary Chavelita Dunne, unknown

112 Mary Chevilita Dunne (George Egerton) by Walter Benington, for Elliott & Fry, chlorobromide print, © National Portrait Gallery, London

113 James Phelan, Library of Congress

113 Pittsburgh, 19th century, Library of Congress

115 An early view of Pittsburgh railway, Library of Congress

116 Hannah Sheehy-Skeffington (1877-1946), photographed c.1916, unknown

116 Frank Skeffington, Wikipedia Commons

117 James Joyce, Wikipedia Commons

118 Sheehy sisters, reproduced from the original held in the Curran Collection at UCD Library Special Collections by kind permission of Helen Solterer

120 Hanna Sheehy and friends, Library of Congress

120 Hanna Sheehy and son, Library of Congress

122 Maud Gonne, Library of Congress

122 William Butler Yeats, by George Charles Beresford © National Portrait Gallery, London

124 Iseult Gonne, © Paula McGloin

125 W. B. Yeats, Library of Congress

126 Maud Gonne, Library of Congress

128 W. B. Yeats, Library of Congress

129 John B Yeats, Portrait of William Butler Yeats, © National Gallery of Ireland

131 James Joyce, Alex Ehrenzweig, Wikipedia Commons

133 Nora Barnacle, Wikipedia Commons

135 Nora Barnacle, Wikipedia Commons

137 Contemporary portrait of Joyce and Barnacle by John Nolan, © John Nolan

138 George Moore, Wikipedia Commons, Project Gutenberg

138 Lady Maud Cunard, unknown

140 John Millington Synge, Wikipedia Commons

142 Molly Allgood, unknown

143 Thomas MacDonagh, Irish Volunteers, unknown

146 Wikipedia Commons

148 Joseph Mary Plunkett, Wikipedia Commons

148 Richmond Barracks, courtesy www.generalmichaelcollins.ie

149 Grace Gifford, unknown

150 Eamonn Ceantt, unknown

151 Women of Cumann Na mBan, unknown

153 A First World War recruitment advertisement, Library of Congress

154 Soldiers fighting in the trenches, Library of Congress

155 Soldiers loading shells in the trenches, Library of Congress

156 Postcard, TPL

157 Ezra Pound, © Horst Tappe / Lebrecht Music & Arts

159 Portrait of Iseult Gonne, © National Gallery of Ireland

160 Olga Rudge, Yale Collection of American Literature, Beinecke Rare Book and Manuscript Library

161 Francis Stuart, © T. Martinot / Lebrecht Music & Arts

162 Peadar Kearney, Wikipedia Commons

163 Brendan Behan, Wikipedia Commons

164 Michael Collins, www.generalmichaelcollins.com

164 Kitty Kiernan, unknown

164 Harry Boland, unknown

166 Harry Boland, Library of Congress

168 The first Dáil, Library of Congress

169 Michael Collins, www.generalmichaelcollins.com

170 Maud Kiernan wedding, Michael Collins, www.generalmichaelcollins.com

172 Michael Collins, www.generalmichaelcollins.com

173 Kitty Kiernan, www.generalmichaelcollins.com

174 Michael Collins ambush, TPL

175 Liam O'Flaherty, publicity photo from The Informer, Military Service Publishing Co. / Stackpole Publishing

177 Liam O'Flaherty, The Informer, Military Service Publishing Co. / Stackpole Publishing

178/181 Dame (Jean) Iris Murdoch by Tom Phillips, 1984–1986 © National Portrait Gallery, London

179 Frank Thompson, courtesy www.specialforcesroh.com

182 Erwin Schrödinger, Wikipedia Commons

184 Schrödinger crater, NASA

185 Patrick Kavanagh, unknown

185 Hilda Moriarty, unknown

186 Patrick Joseph Kavanagh, by Patrick Swift, © estate of Patrick Swift / National Portrait Gallery, London

187 Maureen O'Hara, Wikipedia Commons

189 Film-maker John Ford on set of the film Seven Women in 1965, Mary Evans

190 Elizabeth Bowen by Howard Coster, © National Portrait Gallery, London

192 Charles Ritchie, Library of Congress

193 J. G. Farrell, Snowdon, Vogue / Camera Press

196/199 Hugh Leonard, © Gerray Sweeny, CORBIS

Every effort has been made to contact copyright holders not mentioned here. If there have been any omissions, we will be happy to rectify this in a reprint.